CELESTE WALTERS is the author of playscripts for children
and adults, novels and picture story books for young readers,
texts on developmental drama and the writing of eulogies,
and three books of whimsical verse for all ages. She has also
written five highly acclaimed novels for young adults. Celeste
has been a teacher, an art gallery director, a children's theatre
producer and a university lecturer. Currently she divides her
time between Melbourne and country New South Wales where
she writes, cares for newborns and entertains groups at the
University of the Third Age.

ANNE SPUDVILAS is a multi-award-winning illustrator of
children's books and an established portrait painter who also
works as a courtroom artist for the Melbourne media. Her
first picture book, *The Race*, was awarded the Crichton Award
for Illustration and Children's Book Council of Australia
(CBCA) Honour Book. In 2000 she won CBCA Picture
Book of the Year for *Jenny Angel*, and her latest picture book,
The Peasant Prince, has received the NSW and Queensland
Premiers' Literary Awards, the Australian Book Industry Award
and CBCA Honour Book. Anne lives and works in Melbourne.

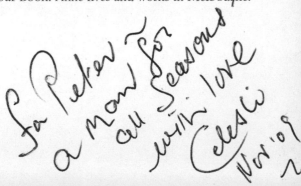

A Certain Music

Celeste Walters

illustrated by Anne Spudvilas

WOOLSHED PRESS
An Imprint of Random House Australia

A Woolshed Press book
Published by Random House Australia Pty Ltd
Level 3, 100 Pacific Highway, North Sydney NSW 2060
www.randomhouse.com.au

First published by Woolshed Press in 2009

Addresses for companies within the Random House Group can be found at
www.randomhouse.com.au/offices.

National Library of Australia
Cataloguing-in-Publication Entry

Author: Walters, Celeste
Title: A certain music / Celeste Walters; illustrator, Anne Spudvilas
ISBN: 978 1 74166 333 4 (pbk.)
Target Audience: For children
Other Authors/Contributors: Spudvilas, Anne, 1951–
Dewey Number: A823.3

Cover and internal design and typesetting by Sandra Nobes, Toucan Design
Printed and bound by Griffin Press, South Australia

Random House Australia uses papers that are natural, renewable and recyclable products and
made from wood grown in sustainable forests. The logging and manufacturing processes are
expected to conform to the environmental regulations of the country of origin.

10 9 8 7 6 5 4 3 2 1

The child isn't like other children. Whether this is because of some intellectual or emotional difference, nobody knows. Of course, one day they will. One day they will give the condition a label, a particular code mark. But this is 1823. In consequence, after much muttering and musing and shaking of heads, she is simply pronounced odd.

Neither do they know — how can they — that this child will live for all time in every town and city of every country in the world where one might hear a certain music.

This is her story. A story that begins in the Vienna Woods.

for Rena

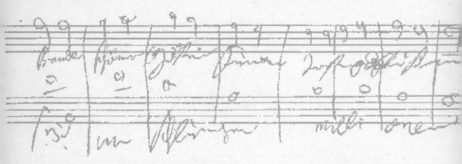

PART I

The Man in the Woods

One

She was a child of nine who knew no friend. An all-watching child who viewed the play of others in the square; who read in their secret whispering descriptions of herself. She knew the reason for this. She couldn't follow the rules. She misinterpreted signals. Worse, she didn't know how to play. Everything she did was either too much or not enough. Whatever she did, it was wrong.

So she listened for other whispering and found it in the water that bubbled from the fountain, in the rustle of needles in the conifer beyond her window, in the distant call of the early morning vendors as they set up their stalls in the market place. And she would wander further from the small cottage by the granary, to where the wind roams free and where the trees grow tall and tight together. And it was there that she came upon a tree whose ladder-like branches rose up and up.

The tree stood in the Vienna Woods, together with the maples and the elms, the beeches and the oaks. Now, settled high in a fork of its branches, she could hear the

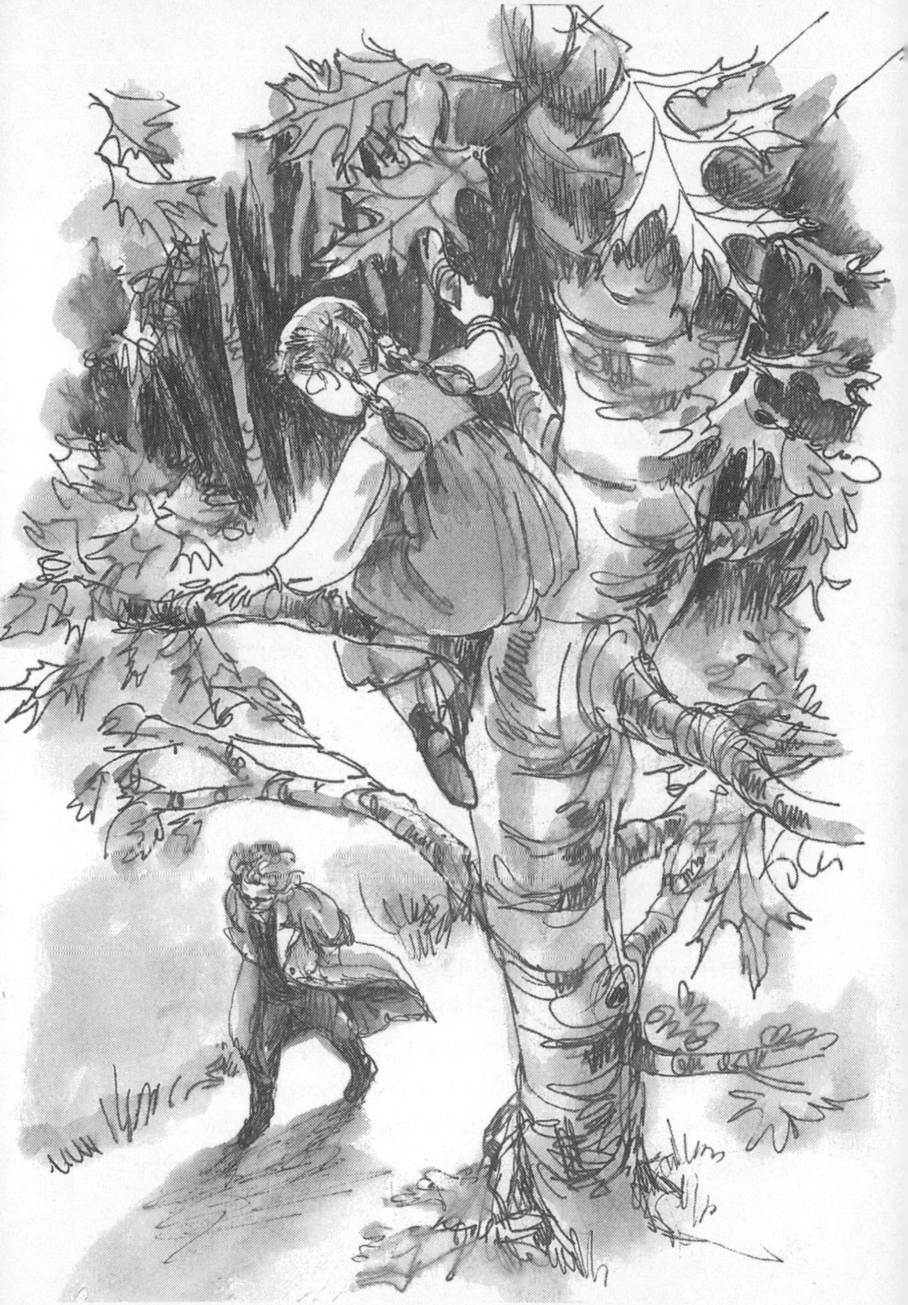

whispering of early morning, see the carts trundling into the marketplace, the raggedy boys with hoops scooting behind their turning wheels, trace with a finger the distant ruins of Rauhenstein still cloaked in mist; follow the mayor bustling his way to the town hall as the clock struck the hour.

Soon sunlight would streak from the heavens, like the picture in her *Stories from the Bible*. With sunlight would come people, walking and talking and laughing, and calling each other by name. The morning would become a different colour and shape, and mask the sounds of silence.

Then on one particular day something broke the silence. The child looked left and right, and behind her. The sound was sharp, made, perhaps, by some animal. But what? And a strange looking creature had appeared out of nowhere and was striding along a path. It was a man. His head was down as though he was searching the ground for something; his hands were behind his back. The child eased into the fork of the tree. The man veered off the path and took another leading in her direction. She eased further into the fork. Now she could see him clearly. The man was small and rugged. His hair was the colour of the maple leaf in autumn and it grew wildly from his head in a tangle of curls. His clothes were shabby, his boots muddy, and around his neck he wore a rag. His unfastened frockcoat, long and blue in colour, billowed behind him as he walked. He reminded her of the stunted waterbirds with the blue-black wings that roam the lake. Suddenly he stopped and lifted his head. The man's face was red, his skin pock-marked. He stood beneath her tree and stared into the sky. Still staring, he started to move his hand up and down, then brought it to his lips and began to tap with one finger...

In the fork of the tree the child's foot was stuck. As she tried to wrench it free, a branch cracked. The man turned. He didn't seem to register seeing a child in a tree. It was as though he was looking at her but through her to something else, something deep and far away. Now he was scrabbling in his pockets. The child watched as he took out a thick carpenter's pencil and a notebook and started filling the page with strange markings. From time to time he'd stop, move his hand backwards and forwards across his chest. And scribble on.

Now from this way and that came hurrying and scurrying and laughing and calling. As a giggling trio pounded across his path, the man let out an explosion of words, raw and terrible...

There was only one the watcher in the tree could hear clearly as, his frockcoat ballooning behind him, he raged back in the direction from which he had come.

The word *cruel*.

Two

In narrow streets by the granary are the cottages where the poor people live. Those who work in factories, who thresh the grain, or those who, for a few Kreutzers, tinkle away on their barrel organs or perform conjuring tricks in the square.

In one such dwelling the child swished a broom over a stone floor. From time to time she'd hear the clip-clop of hooves and go to the window, and watch the cart taking grain to the granary creak up the hill. She put away the broom, pulled up the coverlet on her trundle bed, patted it straight, propped her doll against the pillow, and with a flick of her sleeve, brushed dust from the small chest of drawers that held her clothes. On the bench in the kitchen was a note. The child read, 'Collect eggs from Frau Weiss.' She stood on a box, reached to the mantel and took money from a jar. With the Kreutzers in the pocket of her pinafore, she clipped the door behind her, and set out.

Even before she reached the end of the street she

could hear the rustic tumult of the market. Her pace quickened. Her wariness also. If her mother were a home mother and not a working one she would watch where her child wandered and frown and shake her finger and warn her of the charlatans and swindlers who lurked at every street corner.

She hugged the coins in her pinafore tighter. But the colours and sounds of the market were so rich and wonderful no imagining was needed to conjure them up.

She ran towards it, thinking if she were lucky a puppet show would be on in one of the caravans parked near the column.

In the square she wandered from one excitement to the next, pausing at a man in yellow with performing dogs who sat and begged and shook hands and bowed to much applause. Further along a man and a woman waltzed together to a tune played on a squeaky fiddle. And the sound joined with other sounds; with the calling of hawkers with their trays of trinkets and of vendors selling sausage and cheeses and fruit.

And as she circled, the child was aware that others were circling too, were calling her name, were jumping out from behind things to mimic her lisp.

'Yeth yeth yeth,' they crowed.

And she smiled, hoping they would smile. But they never did.

She hurried towards Frau Weiss and the eggs.

'And one extra for you,' the woman said.

'Danke, Frau Weiss,' the child replied and handed over the money.

'The child's turning into a street urchin,' remarked a woman on the next stall who sold cheese.

'What can the mother do?' hissed back the other. 'He drinks . . . '

'Poor wretch.'

'Useless bum . . . Eggs! Fresh eggs! Eggs laid today!'

The child's ears were sharp. She didn't wait for the next puppet show but hurried away, leaping, as she went, out of the path of a coach being driven at high speed. On past the workhouse and along the darkening network of narrow streets she ran, clutching the eggs in her pinafore with care. A man was moving along the street towards her. They both stopped in front of the small paling fence with the wooden gate.

'Eggs,' she said, opening her pinafore.

Her father smiled. He took her hand but his look didn't reach her eyes. Those who mocked her had the same look. That of a guilty thing . . .

Three

They talked together by the rustling conifer, away from the child. When they came inside her mother looked older, her father, unhappy. Eggs were eaten in silence and the world grew dark.

In her trundle bed by the window the child feigned sleep, listened with ears pricked to the muffled sounds that came from the big bed. From time to time her mother would cough hard and long and spit into a handkerchief. 'The fibres get up your nose,' she'd laugh. Though how fibres could get up your nose was a mystery to the child, regardless of what work in the paper-making factory her mother was doing.

'You should never have left the forge...' her mother was saying.

'Bad company – ' she heard her father mumble.

'You were weak.'

'I'm sorry.'

Her mother went on. 'A clerk's pay is hard to live on, but with mine and the few Kreutzers you get at the tavern we could manage, just. But now...'

'I'm sorry.'

'They will not get away with this...'

'It was my fault.'

'It was. But they knew what they were doing – ' There came another bout of coughing and spitting. The child pulled the coverlet over her ears. She didn't want to hear any more. This was a place of love. Her mother and father loved each other and they loved her equally. But another face of the world had been brought in...

Suddenly she heard the mattress creak. Her mother was getting up, had taken her shawl from the doorknob and was creeping out.

'Where are you going?' came from the bed.

The only reply was that of the door being shut.

From her trundle bed, the child, eyes watching and wide, stared from the window into the night. Like a genie who pops from a bottle to cast a spell, so the moon, now full, had cast a spell over the night and stamped the world in silver. Silver flowers in silver pots spilled from silver windows. The rooftops, and trees beyond, Herr Neumann's dog asleep at his door, the filigree of fruit trees – all shone in silver. And above the tree-tops, stars twinkled in a silver sky.

It was magic. She would have sneaked outside, but eyes from the big bed were awake and watching.

She studied fingers resting on the sill that had turned silver and listened for her mother.

# Four

The woman whipped the shawl around her head and took off. She reached the marketplace, now bare of traders, stalls and caravans, of all but the column with its shimmering star and cross of gold. She hurried through the square, and along streets where shadows leered with menace in the moonlight. As she turned a corner she could see an orange glow and, as she got closer, hear the hum of noise. She pushed open the mitred door and entered into a haze of smoke, and the smell of bodies and cheap wine.

The tavern was filled with men mostly but woman too joined in the laughter and the banging of fists on tables. Someone on the stage was attempting to sing.

'Hey, over here.'

'No.'

'Uppity, eh?'

She pushed ahead. The man behind the bar wore a rag around a neck thick as that of a bullfrog.

'Next?'

'How dare you – ' Her voice was trembling.

'What?'

'You knew his weakness yet you paid him in wine . . . '
Her voice was getting stronger, clearer. People at the bar
were staring.

She went on, her sound strong now, 'Shame on you . . .
You get the wine cheap and the more he takes the less you
pay and you ply him with more so you can pay him less;
no more than you would pay a dog to do tricks . . . '

Suddenly the whole place had become silent.

'Shame on you.' The woman swung around. 'Shame on
all of you for you know him, but you watched and said
nothing. Yet you listened. Oh yes, you did that. For who
among you can quote Schiller and Goethe as Otto can?
None of you. And you know it. You know it as you know
his weakness, and you did nothing. Shame on you – on
all of you . . . ' The woman broke into a fit of coughing.
She staggered towards the door as bodies parted to let her
through.

'He wanted it!' yelled the man at the bar.

On the street, the woman sobbed. She drew her shawl
tighter and started back. At the corner she heard the
sound of footsteps behind her. She went faster. The
footsteps went faster, were catching up.

'Wait!'

Her heart was thumping inside her chest, but she
turned and saw, coming closer, the man who had opened
the door as she fled.

'The army is recruiting,' he said. 'In the wars against Napoleon we lost many. The pay is good and – ' he paused, 'there is discipline.'

The woman stood in the watery glow of a gas lamp and hung her head.

'Otto is a lucky man,' he added.

'Oh?'

'To have a woman like you.' The man gave a quick bow and walked back along the street.

In the cottage by the granary the child heard the gate click open. She pulled the coverlet up and fell asleep.

 Five

The day was the colour of butter. Perfect for being with someone whose hand you can hold and hear street musicians play melodies you tap your feet to.

When they got to the cafe in the Kaiserstrasse the players were having a break.

They sat outside and ate cake. The child dropped crumbs.

'The birds will thank you,' remarked her father. He pulled his seat closer. 'I am going away,' he said.

The child turned, questioning with her eyes.

'You shall be very proud of me. You can tell everyone that your papa is in the army, that he wears a jacket with gold buttons. He looks very handsome in his jacket with gold buttons and – ' the man breathed deeply, 'he is happy for he is serving his country which he loves and making his wife and his daughter proud which makes him happier, for he loves them best of all.'

The child tossed cake to a head-bobbing bird. 'When?' she asked.

'Soon.'

'When's soon?'

'The army will teach me things,' her father continued. 'Things I have forgotten that are important. Like the things that you are taught in school are important.'

The child continued to toss crumbs.

The man paused, then, 'When your mother leaves for the factory she believes you are leaving for school. But she is not always right, is she?'

The child is silent.

'The authorities have been to the house. It is the law that you attend the Volkschule until you are ten so that you will continue to learn your letters and numbers.'

'I know my letters and numbers.'

'There are things to learn besides letters and numbers... Just think, you and me, both in places where we are learning things. What a happy thought. Every day we shall think of each other and of the new things we are learning... Imagine that! Think too, *Liebling*, of your mother who worries.'

The musicians had returned and were tuning up.

'The school is on holiday now,' the man pointed out, 'but when it goes back, you will attend. Yes?'

'Yes.'

'Every day?'

'Yes.'

'You say yes but—'

'I promise.'

The quartet had launched into a waltz.

'You are strong,' whispered the man, 'like your mother. You have a beautiful mind, which is a rare thing. And I love you.'

With hands that dropped crumbs the child reached for her father and buried her face in his neck.

Today there was much for the man to do, so when the players were having their next break, father and daughter walked off, one to the clerk's office, the other to the woods.

In the Vienna Woods the maples, the oaks, the elms and the beeches were heralding the march of winter as the last of their leaves twirled like dancers to the ground.

Today many people were about. They strolled across the grass or sat on rugs under trees with baskets of cheese and wine ... From the fork in the tree the child watched the comings and goings of carts carrying families of picnickers, and here and there a carriage with fine ladies and men in silk hats would wind along a forest drive. Her eye caught something moving in the distance. It was a funeral. She had observed one before. She loved the black horses with the plumes on their heads that nodded and bowed as they plodded up the hill to the churchyard. This funeral was small, only a handful of people walked behind the carriage draped in black. The child wondered why sad things should look so beautiful.

A hare scuttled by as she jumped to the ground. She wandered on, leapt to catch the dead leaves that rose with the kick of her boot. They crackled underfoot like the sound of rifle fire and an image rose of jackets with gold buttons.

The sun had brought the world out on this festive day. This way and that ladies and gentlemen strolled arm in arm, children in dresses ran with hoops, men in uniform clopped along on horseback, carriages rolled, carts rattled, and from somewhere came the sound of marching music. People were moving in that direction.

The child went the other way. There were many ways to get to the cottage by the granary and taking this route she could play games as she went, asking herself who lived in what house, who they lived with and what – at that moment of passing – they were doing.

The first street she took was empty. She walked on, past houses with long windows, where chimneys poked from rooftops and boxes with flowers stood at the door. Suddenly she stopped. The house was like any other, but coming from it was the most beautiful sound she had ever heard. It wasn't like that of the wind in the conifer, or the bubble of water in the fountain. The sound conjured up no image. She only heard the music.

The door was open. She peered inside.

The man seated at the piano was the man in the woods with the wild hair. Suddenly he stopped, picked up his pencil, marked a page and played on. Again he stopped, looked left and right for the pencil, but it had dropped to the floor. As he bent to retrieve it he saw the child standing in the doorway.

'Go!' he roared, flinging his hand wide as though he would strike her. 'Get out. Out! Out! Out!'

She shot away, but didn't leave. Instead she sat on the pavement and listened again for the music.

But it didn't come. Only the man came. He strode from the door, stared briefly at the small figure sitting cross-legged on the ground, and, with his blue frockcoat flapping, stomped off.

As if by magic, street urchins jumped out from nowhere to bark at him.

•   •   •

A smell was coming from the kitchen in the cottage by the granary. A most delicious smell.

The woman inside had let her hair down. It fell in waves to her waist. She was also wearing her best shawl. 'Tonight we are celebrating,' she announced as the child came in. 'We are having meat with potatoes and red cabbage, and wine. Your father is trying on his uniform. And,' delivered in a hushed voice, 'remember to say how handsome he looks.'

In came the soldier-to-be and indeed he did look handsome. Mother and child clapped. The woman embraced her husband. 'And what did the two of you get up to this morning?' she asked.

'We heard music and ate cake.'

The woman turned to her daughter. 'Was it nice – the music?'

'Beautiful,' the child replied.

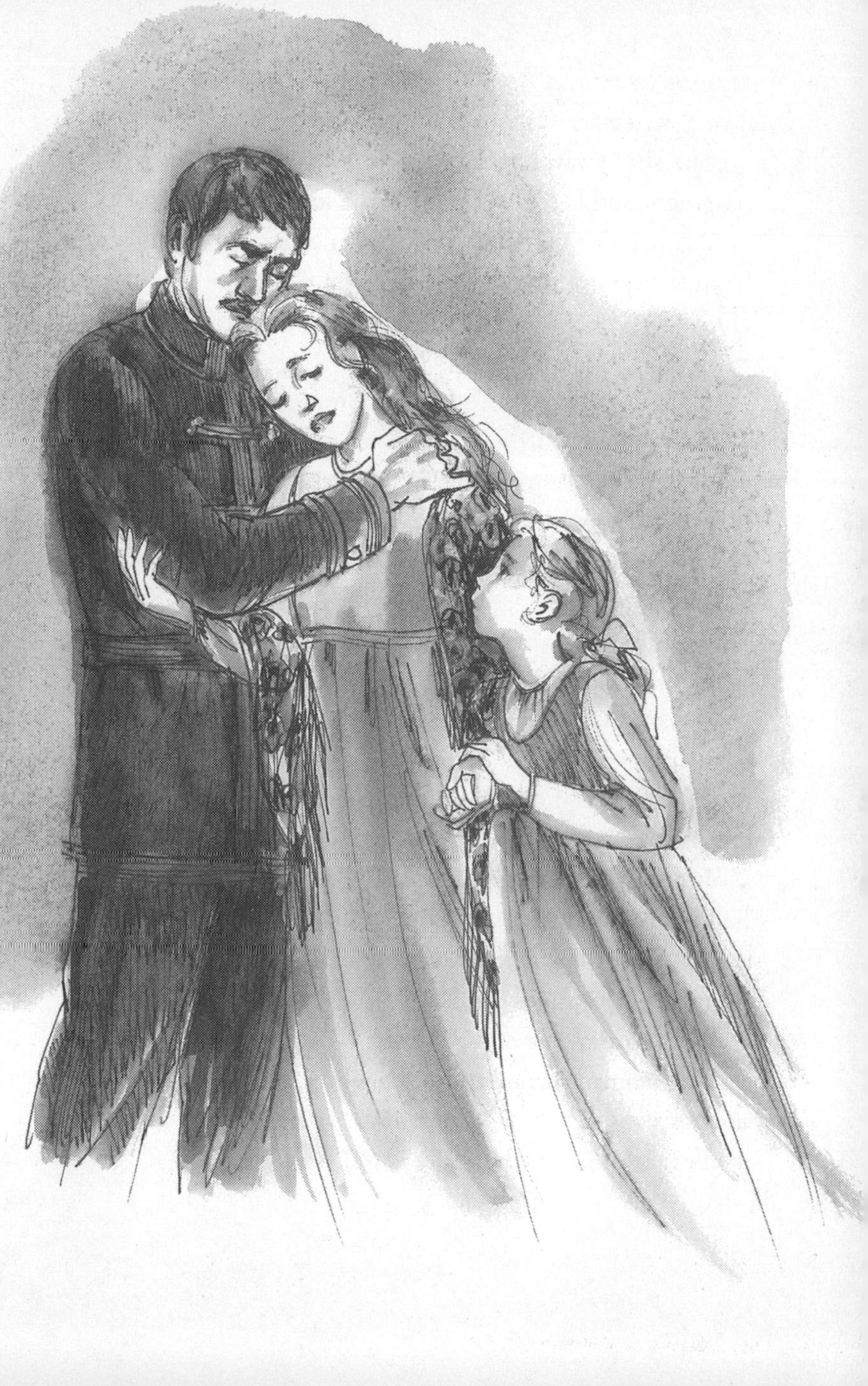

Six

In two days her father would be leaving. Not that there was any front for him to leave for and die in. Napoleon had been defeated and banished to the island of St Helena. But an army still must train ...

'It is good for the mind,' her mother said, 'as well as the body. And – ' she stopped to cough and spit onto the road, 'you and I will eat well and that will be good too.'

It was late afternoon and they were walking home from the factory. Often the child would wait at the great iron gate that led to where old rags as well as straw and grass and the bark from trees were turned into paper.

Today, as she stood waiting, a group from the Volkschule rounded the corner and were idling their way towards her. She turned her face to the gate.

'Her *Vater*'s a drunkee.'

'A fish *Vater*.'

A stone whizzed past her head. The boys threw stones but the words the girls threw hurt harder. A man on his horse clopped by and all four ran.

The child remained at the gate as a group of older women streamed across the yard. She caught snatches of their talk as they pressed together through the gate.

'She's dying – that's what I heard – '

'Can't breathe.'

'It's the lime – '

'How is it we're not all sick then?'

'We might be – '

'All of us might be – '

'Blind like Iris – '

'That was an accident.'

A second wave of workers appeared. Her mother among them.

'What's the lime?' The child wanted to know. The woman bent down. 'I haven't had my kiss yet,' she said.

'What's the lime?'

'Things are used to make paper – like caustic lime ... '

'It's bad.'

'Who said that?'

'Somebody ... '

The woman sighed. 'Frau Schultz has been taken to the infirmary and everybody's panicking ... ' She opened her bag and took out a ham roll. 'Here.'

'That's your lunch.'

'I wasn't hungry.'

They walked on.

'There's accidents,' the child remarked through a mouthful of roll.

'Don't worry. I'm careful.'
Eyes followed a cart creak up the hill to the granary.
'Its wheel is wobbling,' the woman said.

Seven

As the moth returns to the flame, so the child returned to the house in the Reinerstrasse.

And again the door was open. But today the sounds were different. They came in waves and spurts and at times with long breaks in-between. Often the man would crash down on the keys with both hands and the chords were harsh and angry.

The child stood to the left of the door and listened. A long silence followed. She peeked around the door. The man was at the piano, his hands poised above the keys. He sat very still, for what, to the child, seemed an eternity. Then he played.

The sound he made was more beautiful than before, more beautiful than anything she had ever heard. The man, without pausing, suddenly turned his head as though he sensed someone was watching. 'What do you see?' he said.

What did he mean, 'What do you see?' The child didn't know. She thought of the tree in the woods and of the million colours and shapes she saw from the fork in its branches. Nothing was right. There were no images to describe what she heard, not even in the flow of the fountain or the wind in the conifer. And then suddenly a picture did form, of a night when she had looked from the window and seen the world cast in silver.

'Moonlight,' she said.

The man continued to play. 'Write it,' he ordered.

The child peered inside. Near the door was a small table and on it stood a notebook and a pencil. She crept towards it, wrote, crept back, sat on the step and went on listening.

Finally the man lifted his hands from the keys. He got up, grabbed the blue frockcoat that was lying on the floor and, pulling the door behind him, strode out. The child watched him pass. He was taller than she first thought and, with his coat billowing behind him and his long hair sticking out from under an old hat, he made a weird shape. People stopped and stared and nodded their heads.

The man walked in the direction of the woods. The child followed. It was a day of biting air and sweeping mist.

He paced along a path strewn with leaves and flanked by oaks. He came to a seat and sat hunched in the mist turned rain, his head in his hands.

The child peered from behind a maple and waited, but he didn't move. Still she waited. She came closer. Now she stood before him.

Again, as if sensing the presence of someone, he raised his eyes. 'You!'

From somewhere came the distant clanging of a bell. The child turned.

'Tell me what you hear,' he said.

'A goat is lost,' replied the child.

The man shook his head from side to side and looked down. Then he spoke. 'You have heard something. Perhaps the distant sound of a bell, or the calling of a bird, and I have heard nothing. When someone has heard a shepherd singing, or a flute being played, again I have heard nothing . . .'

Now rain fell in thick globs, it splashed onto his boots, dropped from his hat, from her braids, like a metronome's beat.

The child studied the man's face, the jutting lower lip, the eyes that glowed. Silently she stood before him.

'Why?' he barked.

Silence.

'Why do you follow me?'

Silence.

'Have you nowhere to go that you sit on my doorstep?' The child said nothing.

'I cannot work when people watch. It sends me mad.' Still silence.

'You sit hour after hour. Why? For what?'

At the child's feet was a stick. She picked it up and in the wet earth beneath a giant oak, wrote, 'The music.'

Eight

That night the man dreamed. On a crumpled bed in crumpled clothes he dreamed: his hat, his frockcoat and boots, like pieces of a jigsaw, tossed upon the floor.

He is four. He is wearing a white shirt and yellow britches. The shirt has frills. He is playing in the square. A group has gathered. He doesn't have to tell his fingers where to go or how long to rest upon the strings. They know. The violin is a quarter size, the smallest. Another Mozart, they're whispering. His father smiles.

The boy loves this little instrument. It sings for him. But now his violin is gone from its peg in the hall, and the bow with it, and his father is saying that from now on he will play only the piano. And the sound he makes is slurred with drink. The boy says nothing, for there is violence behind the words, and fear too. And both come from knowing poverty and sickness and despair...

Now the scene changes. It is dark, it is late, well after midnight.

He is five. He's in bed, he's shivering, it's winter and the room is damp. He curls into a ball and pulls the coverlet higher; blocks out the rattle of his mother's breath, her coughing and gasping, hears voices, boots lurching on the stairs ... The cover is ripped away. In the dark, his father's voice is thick with drink. 'Downstairs, you hear?'

'Please, *Vater* — '

A hand reaches out as if to strike. Instead it yanks the small shivering body from the bed. 'Now!'

'Yes, *Vater*.'

He is five. He pulls the cover around his nightshirt and creeps along the cold stone floor, descends the stairs, sees his breath rise like autumn mist in the stuttering candlelight.

They stand before the last dying embers in the grate, his father and Herr Pfeiffer his friend, who is to be the boy's teacher. Both are red-eyed and watchful.

His father points a wavering finger at the piano. 'Start playing!'

He is five. He sits at the piano. His teeth are chattering, it's the cold, the fear, it's the shame of it ...

'What shall I play, *Vater*?'

The man lurches into a chair, tips a second one over, 'See how I suffer! Imagine Mozart asking "What shall I play"?'

The small boy places his hands on the keys, hands that are stiff with the cold. The sound they make is cold ...

Fists crash upon the table, a glass shatters. 'You dare to humiliate me —'

'I'm cold, *Vater* — '

'Play, damn you!'

'Please, *Vater* — '

The man staggers up, sinks down, clasps his head in his hands. 'Another Mozart, they said. Fools . . . fools and idiots . . .'

The small figure hunched at the piano closes his eyes and starts to play. Only music can take away the cold, only music can relieve the hunger, and the pain. He plays on. When finally he stops, the visitor has left and his father is asleep at the table.

He puts down the lid and creeps upstairs.

The dreamer stirred, poured from the bowl of wine that stood on the sideboard, drank deeply, dreamed on . . .

Now he is standing in front of a carved door hewn from oak. He is wearing a blue frockcoat. It has gold buttons and is trimmed with lace. Frills of lace flow from his throat and also from his wrists. His britches are the colour of chocolate, and there are gold buckles on his shoes. His hair explodes in curls of red. His face, by contrast, is pale.

He is seven and a half and is about to give his first public concert. His father is by his side.

It's like a palace. The boy has never seen such a room, with its rich red carpet, its walls of mirrors, its magnificent paintings, the enormous deep-hanging circlets of fluttering light. And the women and the men, so elegant in their silks and laces and gold brocades . . .

The room is full of circle upon widening circle of balloon-backed chairs that face the platform on which stands the piano, all shiny and black.

He is seven and a half.

He moves to it and sits, he adjusts the chair, hears silence fall.

Now there is only the music. He places his hands on the keys.

And begins.

• • •

The man pulled himself up and stood long in the dark. He paced to the window and back, to the window again, sloshed down wine, whipped up a sheet of manuscript that was lying on the floor, lit a candle, and in a frenzy started to write and play and play and write. But the sound he made was full of pain, and had no purpose, but to ignite pain.

In the darkness of his lonely room he lifted up his head. And howled.

Long he stood. Then once again he went to the piano and began to play. Now the sound was different. He was seven and a half again, in that wonderful room with its walls of mirrors. Over and over he played what he had performed on that evening when he was seven and a half ...

He played until the white light of morning leaked into the room. He threw open the door and went on playing.

From time to time he glanced into the street ...

Nine

Beneath the conifer that grew beyond her window, the child sat, a sheet of paper in her hand. From time to time she'd look up as the body of needles above her rippled in a rush of wind.

Eight days had passed since her father had embarked upon his new life, and now word had come and with it a page for her.

'... I am sleeping well, *Liebling*,' he wrote, 'for the day begins early and there are many things to do, and you will be happy to know that your papa is fit and has been praised for his diligence and cooperation.

'Also I have a friend. His name is Manfred and he is the son of a farrier. I was a blacksmith for a long time, and he and I talk about axles and rims for wheels, and the shoeing of horses – how very dull, I hear you say, but it makes me happy to talk about things I know of, and it's good to have a friend.

'Here is something that will make you smile. At the

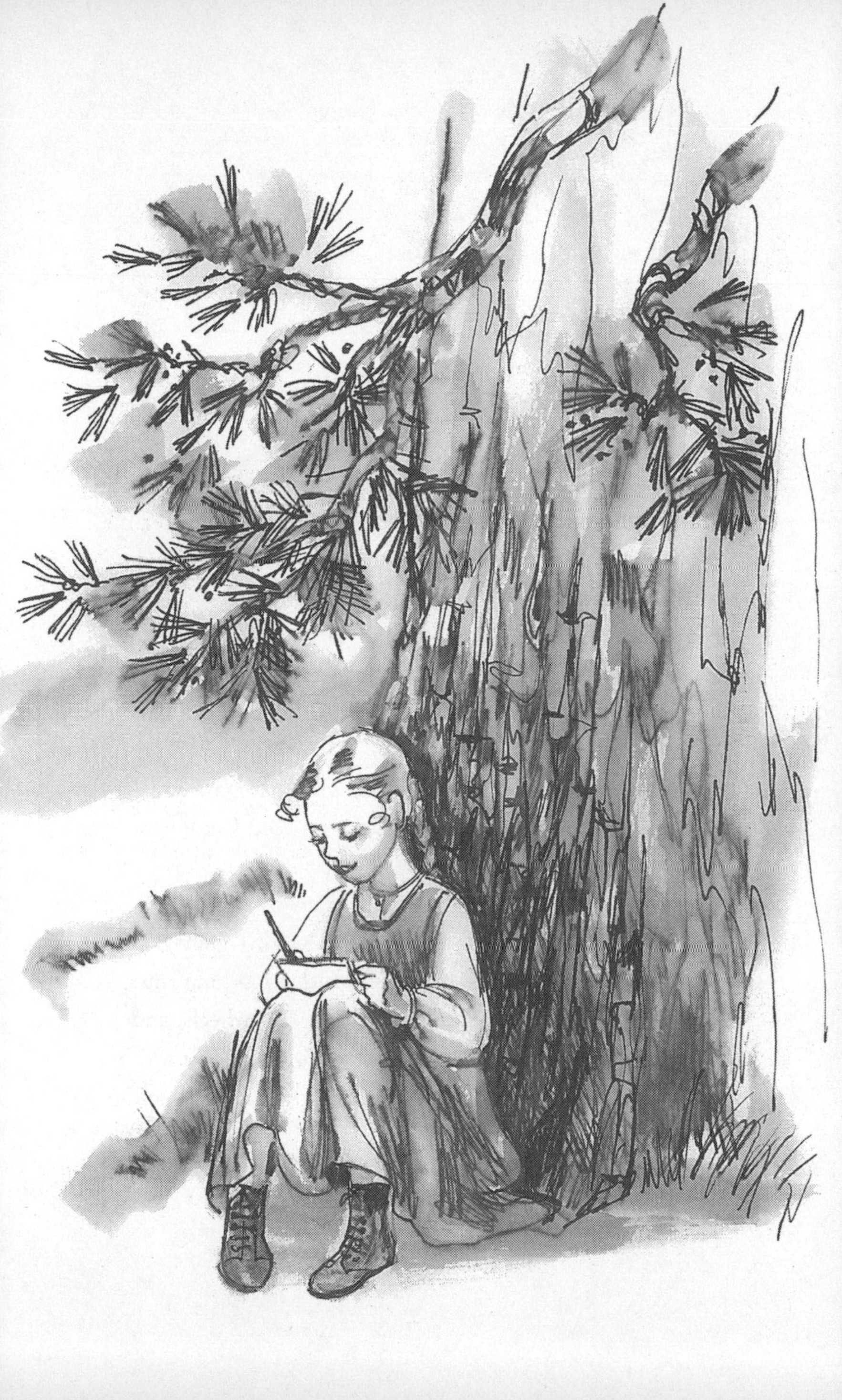

garrison we have a pet, a red squirrel. He has taken
up residence in the elm tree on the edge of the parade
ground. We feed him grains and bits of fruit, and nuts
when we get them. He is quite tame and on one occasion
he lined up with us on parade. It was difficult for everyone
not to smile. His name is Fritz.

'I have sent *Mutti* some money and a little extra to buy
something for my best girl ...'

The words concluded with a plea to keep helping her
mother, enjoying the last days before school goes back
and holding him close to her heart ...

The child went into the house and returned with paper
and her box of crayons.

She would draw a picture of the conifer. She hoped
she could suggest the swaying of its needles in the wind.

It would make him feel he was home ...

Ten

Now the winds of winter swept through the Vienna
Woods. The elms and the maples, the beeches and the
oaks were bare, their leaves sunk deep into the earth.

Soon the child would return to school, so now
when night fell she would plan the following day with
care. And today she would relive a time that would remain
with her for the rest of her life; the time she had taken
a different path home and had heard the music.

From the fork in the tree she stared into a filigree
of branches, traced webs that spiders spin like Frau
Neumann's lace work. She looked towards Rauhenstein
blanketed in mist, watched carts trundling into the
marketplace, the toing and froing of vendors across
the square.

She jumped down. The earth made a squishing
sound beneath her boots while above, the sky hung
heavy with cloud.

She started out, though now the houses with
long windows, where boxes of flowers stood and

chimneys poked from rooftops, were carved in her memory.

Once again the door to his house was open. The sound coming from it seemed to fill the street.

'I performed this when I was seven and a half,' the man shouted. The child came closer. 'In a place with walls of mirrors. The Elector of Cologne was there, imagine that!'

The child grinned.

Along the street people were running. The man jumped up. 'I too must feel the air against my skin; rejoice in the wonders of God's garden!... Let the devil play what he will...'

The child heard the last mumbled words but their meaning was lost to her. She watched as the man whipped up his frockcoat and hat and charged to the door.

Along the street people were running, but it wasn't to rejoice in God's garden. A man had fallen under the wheels of a carriage and been crushed to death. The crowd had blocked the road. Someone was attempting to calm the horses.

'He was driving like a madman,' yelled a voice.

'Poor thing had no hope.'

A woman was being pushed to the front. The crowd went silent. All was quiet but for the scream.

The man saw but heard nothing. The child wondered if it would be worse or better to see such a thing and not to hear it. She studied the hand, hanging beneath a grubby frill at her side. How strange it is, she thought, for hands to make sounds like that and look like everybody else's.

She tugged gently on the thumb and the man moved away.

In tangles of mist they walked towards the woods and through the woods where the mist was thick and the only sound the squelching of boots in damp earth. And as they went the child slipped her hand into the pocket of the frockcoat by her side.

In that way and in silence they went ...

leven

At the window the child stood, watched drops like pellets fall from the roof, drip upon puddles; heard the rhythm of the rain.

A horse pulling a cart clip-clopped by; spray rose and hissed...

She set about sweeping the floor and fixing her bed. She checked the pail her mother had left outside the door. There was water enough to wash the dishes — also a cloth or two and a few things of her own. She hummed to herself as she went about her chores. Then she took her coat from its peg, wound a scarf around her head and set out.

Over puddles she jumped, splashed into others, flicked rain from her nose. Came to the square, watched rain splatter on covered caravans and carts and people in hoods hurry this way and that with their heads down.

She skipped on, crossed the tiny parkland where a flock of waterbirds had gathered, and turned into the Reinerstrasse.

She could hear sound coming from the house before she reached it, and as she got closer it grew louder and louder; it swept into the street and through the street as though it would rise to the very heavens and send stars crashing to earth.

The child huddled by a neighbour's wall, heard screaming, smashing, the thundering of boots on wood – him.

'...Copy the score exactly, I said. *As I have written it down,* I said. And the fools and idiots have done the opposite. They've done it on purpose. Yes, the treacherous dogs, they have done it on purpose! That I have to deal with such imbeciles, such cretins and half-wits!' Something smashed. 'Music? They know nothing of music! How can one describe beauty to barbarians! If it's not copied exactly, *exactly*, as I wrote it, the speed will not be right. And if the speed is not right – Oh God, God, must I suffer this ignominy...It is because of the singing. Yes. They fear it as they fear anything that is not tried and familiar and predictable. As the swine in the sty knows nothing more than its feed and its filth and the stench of its own excrement...'

Now in the street, wind was blowing. People clung to shawls and hats. Leaves rose and fell swirling to their gutter graves. Suddenly the door to the house, which had been ajar, blew open. The child listened, heard nothing. She moved closer.

The man was standing in a mess of clothes and food

and papers and smashed china. Suddenly he swung around and charged at the child, his eyes wild with torment. 'Get out!' he screamed. 'Away from me! What are you, some devil sent to haunt me, to drive me mad! Out of my sight, do you hear. What would you know of beauty...I tell you, get out! Out! Out of my sight!'

The child stepped back, tripped, fell, scrambled up, slumped against rough brick, pulled her coat tighter, heard her breath, the beat of her heart.

Long she stood, and stared into the cobblestone street, saw the man rush from the house without his coat...

She tried to think of what to do and where to go. But all she could hear was a voice screaming, 'Out! Out of my sight!' She was bewildered, she couldn't understand it. But strangely, what she felt was not fear. Only confusion.

A pebble whizzed by her head. Raggedy boys from the Volkschule, like tigers, were prowling...The child pressed her head to the brickwork, felt a presence...

The man stood there. His hair, his shirt, were wet. 'Ah,' he murmured, 'I have made you cry. I'm sorry... I am mad, you see. Brutal.' He moved closer, drew a finger across the small cheek, wiped away a tear, 'A child is precious, *eine kleine Blume* – a little flower...You must blame my head, the ringing in my ears that drives me mad...And the other. Always the other...I'm sorry, I'm sorry...'

He moved towards his door, then turned and beckoned. 'Come,' he said. 'I will make you forgive me.'

In the room shards of china and ripped sheets of manuscript rose at the kick of his boot. The child followed.

He drew the small table that held his 'conversation book' into the centre of the clutter, set a chair at it and began rummaging through the debris for his coat that was lying on the floor. 'Here,' he cheered, and held up a block of chocolate, which he began breaking into bits. 'Like a princess, you shall sit and eat, and I shall play for you.'

The child sat and ate.

'I shall play my "Ode to Joy",' announced the man. Then, 'Tell me, what is an ode?'

The child shook her head.

'A poem. Or song. If one is to eat chocolate one must learn a new word. That is the rule.'

He began to play.

The child paused in her eating. This sound was different again. And joy was the right, the perfect word, to picture it. To the child it was as though all the things that make for happiness had been put into a bottle; the cork pulled, and they had exploded upon the world.

The man turned in his playing. 'Well?'

The child nodded. 'Yes,' she mouthed.

The man started to play again, but suddenly there was a knock at the door. He got up. In the pale sunshine that now coloured the street, the man and his visitor talked.

The child contemplated the mess. She got up. A bowl had been broken and a plate. She collected the pieces and took them into the kitchen, where food and the remains of meals lay unwashed and congealing. Untouched on a plate were slices of ham, cheese and pickle.

She returned to the room, picked up bits of food that were lying on the floor, everything except the papers stamped with the strange markings. She shook out the frockcoat and hat and hung them on a peg in the small bedroom. The room smelt. The covers on the bed dripped to the floor and the chamber pot was full.

Had she been on her own she would have emptied it. She would have drawn water from the pump in the street and cleaned up the kitchen.

On the sideboard a candle was stuttering. It had burnt to the wick, and grease had spilled onto the floor. As she blew it out the man came in.

He didn't seem to notice the change in the room but held up six fingers. 'Six weeks,' he said. 'They have six weeks to get it right. I, on the other hand, have got it right already.' He grinned. The child grinned back and pointed to the plate of food she'd brought from the kitchen.

'When I am working I forget to eat.' The man sifted through papers strewn across the floor. 'They say no singing, but are they right?' He straightened up. '*Are they right?*'

The child shook her head.

There came a roar of laughter. 'You're a strange little flower, yet you know things – things only old people know, and wise ones too. Where does this wisdom come

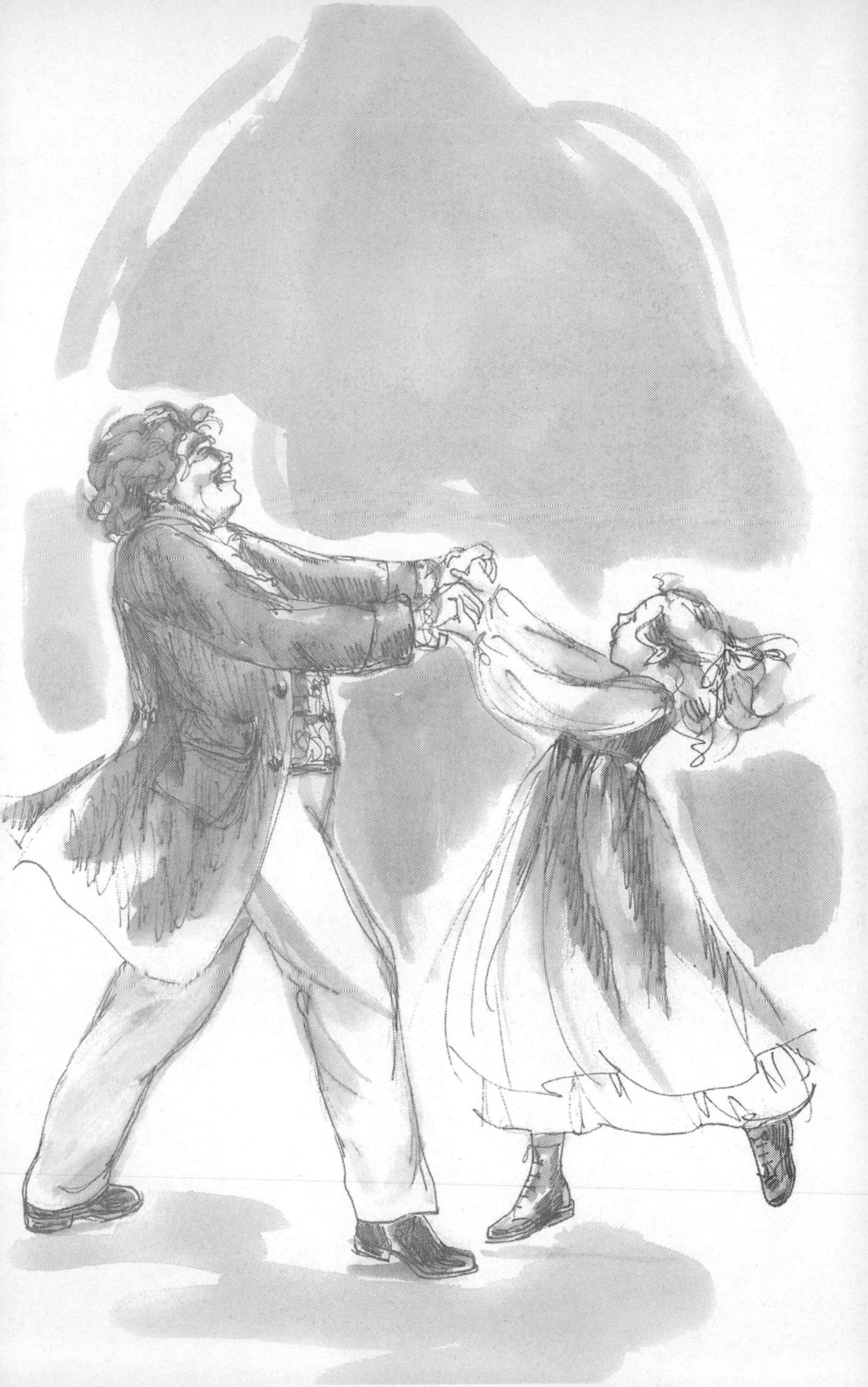

from? What is your secret? What of your parents? Does your mother play?'

The child shook her head.

'Sing?'

Another shake of the head.

'Your father?'

The child went to the conversation book. 'With the army,' she wrote.

'I think — ' the man paused, 'I think that you will bring me luck.' He moved closer, she could taste his breath.

'This is the first time *ever* that there will be voices. There will be a choir. And not only a choir — singers on their own. Four of them. Two on one side and two on the other. What do you think? Am I mad?'

The child shook her head.

'Should there be singing?'

The child nodded hard.

'And so there shall be! There shall be singing, and dancing too!' With that the man leapt to his feet, grabbed the child by the hands and whirled her around and around the room, and together they laughed and whirled and whirled and laughed and the man sang of a song to joy and the child with him...

Twelve

The child danced on. Watched a winter sun slip behind the factory wall, saw the workers in twos and threes and in small groups cross the windswept yard to the main gate. In her heart the dancing paled as she observed how they gestured to each other and kept their voices down.

'Frau Schultz has died,' whispered her mother, 'and they feel anxious.'

In silence they walked in the direction of the square. From time to time the woman stopped, leaned against a fence and spat onto cobblestone. Then, 'She will be buried tomorrow,' she said.

'You don't have to go ...'

'Everyone will. Tomorrow we close early.'

'It's too far.'

'I'll go slowly.'

The child stamped on dead leaves, crunched them underfoot. 'I'll come too,' she said.

'It's not a place for children.'

'I'll wait outside.'

They walked on, huddled together like seabirds against the wind.

'Papa tells me he has sent you a story about a squirrel,' the woman remarked.

'There's a letter?'

'Yes.'

'Is he happy?'

There was a pause.

'What?'

'He has a rash.'

'Where?'

'It's worse on his legs ... It could be the dyes in his uniform ...'

'The lime –?'

'No, not lime.'

'Has he told?' asks the child.

'That may not be a good idea,' her mother replies. 'In any case it's getting better.'

They continued on through the square, then turned into the street by the granary.

The woman said, 'And what did your music man play for you today?'

'His "Ode to Joy".'

'Goodness.'

They reached the small paling fence that enclosed the giant conifer.

'This is the very first time there'll be singing with – with ...' The child stopped.

'With joy?'

'With the music.'

The woman smiled. 'There's always been singing with piano, with violin.'

'It's different.'

'How?'

'I don't know.'

'Is he happy being different?' enquired the woman as she clicked open the gate.

'He's frightened,' replied the child. And walked in.

Thirteen

The following morning was thick with cloud. By late afternoon rain was sweeping in over the hills on the outskirts of the town.

The workers gathered in the square, the women in black with thick shawls and hoods. They stood in silence and tight together; watched rain pitter-patter on the hearse with its wooden box. Black plumes rose and dipped as horses tossed their heads this way and that.

The child took her mother's hand as the carriage moved off. The mourners followed. Along the path and up the hill to the churchyard they toiled.

From time to time the woman would stop and lean on the child until her breath became easier.

By the time they reached the churchyard the squalls had been blown far from the hills and a sallow sun was edging its rays through cloud.

The child watched the women shake their skirts, remove their hoods and follow the box, balanced on the shoulders of four men in mourning dress, into the church.

'I'll wait here,' the child whispered. And added, 'It's all right.'

At the door two women were beckoning. She watched her mother join them, and go in.

She looked around. What she saw reminded her of a painting she'd seen on the wall of a schoolroom, or perhaps imagined that she had. She put her hands to her face, made a hollow square, peered through the frame, saw a church with a bell tower, crosses and angels growing from tangles of grass, trees that spread their branches over dead people in marble.

She moved the frame to the left, watched two birds flit from branch to branch of a spreading oak.

This, thought the child, was what the man meant when he wrote his 'Ode to Joy'. This is what he must have seen and felt.

It was that beautiful.

She began to move, to lift her head, to spread her arms, to rise up . . .

On the gravestones she danced, and as she turned and swirled she sang the song of joy the man had sung in the house along the Reinerstrasse. She had recalled every note without trying or intending to.

Suddenly she stopped. Someone had entered the space.

The child slipped behind a tree and peered out. A woman was standing by a mound of earth. She stood still. There was no sound, no movement, but for a cheeky bird that was hopping backwards and forwards on the chipped wing of an angel.

The child studied the woman. She had seen her before. But where? And then she remembered the scream. And a leg lying under the wheel of a coach.

To the left and to the right, blooms of every colour and shape drooped from marble urns, though in one the flowers were fresh.

Quietly the child dropped to her knees, drew buds of blue and pink, of purple and gold from the urn. Untied a ribbon that held one of her braids and wound it around the stems.

Just as quietly she approached the grassy mound at which the woman was standing and held out the posy. Eyes stared at the flowers, at the child. A hand reached out. '*Danke*,' a voice murmured.

Now came movement. People were spilling out of the church and a bell had begun to toll.

The woman at the mound glanced up, around and began to hurry back along the path.

Dusk was falling as the group from the factory debated whether to stay for the burial or leave. They moved away.

'Are you all right?' The child took her mother's hand, stared into a face the colour of unbaked bread, felt her hand being squeezed.

'Why are some of the graves not covered in stone?' she asked.

'They're probably new and it's still being cut,' replied a woman called Lotti.

'Or the family can't afford it,' chimed in another.

'Look,' cried a third. 'Someone's left a bunch of flowers on that one.'

In the failing light they moved towards the path.

'It's better going downhill,' whispered the child.

'You've lost a ribbon,' her mother replied.

Fourteen

She had gone back to school. The child had promised to, and had crossed her heart.

But now it was different. She had a secret. Something that kept her warm and secure, that wrapped her tight in a turtle shell ... Of course the whispering, the taunting, the small cruelties went on, but not to the same degree. They were losing interest, the panic they read in her eyes when she got it wrong, when she misinterpreted the signals, simply wasn't as it once was. And where is the fun in ridiculing someone because they can't play by the rules, if they don't want to join in anyway?

Added to that the child had a skill for which she was noticed. It was her memory. She could add and subtract faster than anyone. As with her letters, she didn't know how she got there, or what everything meant, she just could do it.

And those who mocked studied her for a response and found, in her eyes, something they couldn't read.

Neither did she spend the time she once did listening

to the sounds that whispered in the fountain and in the needles of the conifer. Of these she was aware, and would always be, but of a far greater importance now was the man at the house in the Reinerstrasse and the sounds he made.

At the end of lessons there would be time to hear some, maybe even the 'Ode to Joy', and if she ran she'd still be able to walk her mother home . . .

As for the man himself, she had learnt whether or not it was wise to remain out of sight, at the door, slip away. Or stay to dance.

The music would tell her . . .

Fifteen

It was Sunday. Sunlight seeped across the floor, painting clothes and shoes and skins of fruit the colour of buttermilk. The child would see to the mess. She had been doing so for some time though the man said nothing. He didn't seem to notice that the chamber pot had been emptied, the bed made and the dishes washed. Though once, as she was packing up, he remarked, 'Most lasted no more than a week.'

Who were 'most'? And why did they not last? The child considered this. She thought of the women at the factory who feared the lime (remember Frau Schultz?); yet they stayed. That sickness came from dirt and things that smelled bad, she knew. That wasn't it. It was his difference that most feared...

The man was still flapping his arms and crowing. 'Forty-six strings will raise the roof beams!' He split into a laugh. 'They think I'm mad. There was a tugging of beards and a great grumbling, but they can laugh all they like, there can be no compromise. The music will not allow it. It's like this – ' Papers fluttered to the floor as he began to sketch.

'See, the violins are here and here, the cellos and violas there; behind them are the flutes, the oboes, the clarinets and bassoons – over here are the trumpets and the horns, at the side are the double basses and at the back the kettle drums and all the other wonderful things that crash and bang and whoop . . . ' A stab at the paper. 'At the front, on the podium with his baton in his hand is the conductor, Kapellmeister Umlauf. Kapellmeister Umlauf knows music – ' A stab at his chest, ' – in here. And – ' more sketching, 'I am on the stage also. Observe the trousers. They are black, my shoes also. The lace at my neck and at my wrists is the colour of coffee. Am I not splendid?'

The child nodded.

'From here the sound will rise to – '

'The roof beams – '

'Exactly.'

'And to the left and to the right and behind also, are the singers. And the audience? They are here in row after row; also in boxes and in galleries that rise up and up and up. You will note that there is not one empty seat . . . But wait! Who is this that sits one two three four rows back from the stage. Can you guess?'

The child shook her head.

'Someone small whose flaxen braids are falling free. She is wearing blue. Why blue? . . . Because her eyes are blue . . . Who can she be?' Still musing, the man moved to the sideboard, took something from a drawer and in the child's hand he placed two tickets. And though the markings on each were a mystery to her, the child knew their meaning.

In the square the town hall clock tolled the hour. In the street a dog began to bark. But the child heard only the beat of her heart.

The man had plucked his coat from the floor and was putting it on. 'You obviously don't want to hear my forty-six strings – observe my splendid trousers . . .' He stood before her. 'Nobody saw it, not Kapellmeister Umlauf, not even the great Haydn. Only you saw the moonlight. Only you . . .' Eyes locked into eyes. There were no words.

Faster than the wind the child ran, her hands spread wide like a ship in full sail. Into the square, through the marketplace, dodging in and out of stalls, between carriages and carts, around hawkers selling fruit, up the street by the granary, faster and faster . . . She flung open the door.

'Look,' she gasped. 'For us!'

Her mother sat at the kitchen table, a jug of something in her hands. A trickle of blood on her bodice writhed like a serpent when she moved. In her lap lay a rag.

'There's forty-six strings and his trousers are black and it'll rise right to the roof beams – not then, at the end – and the colour is blue.'

'Of what?'

'The dress.' The child stopped. 'There's blood – '

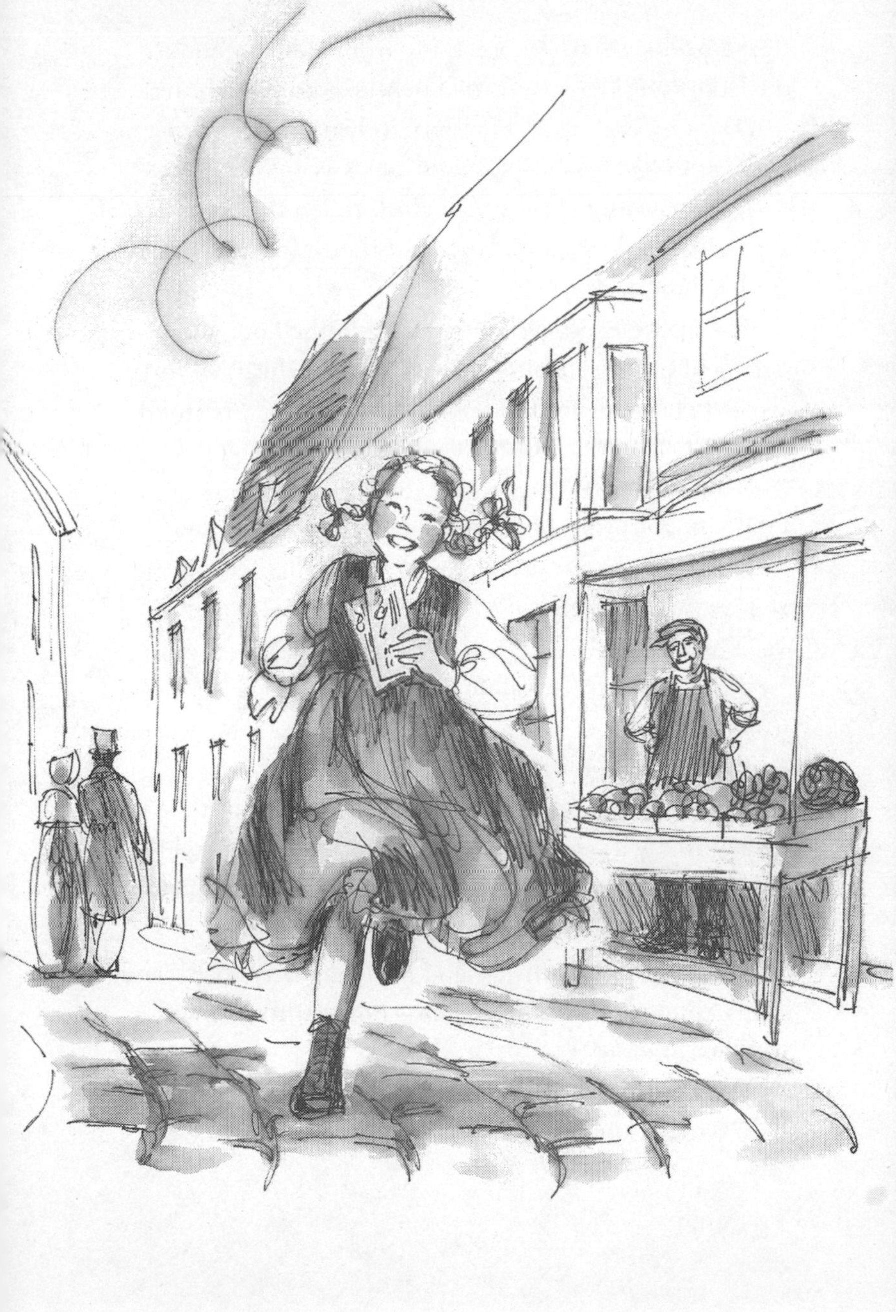

'Coughing, that's all...'

'In two weeks, in fourteen days, in 168 waking up hours...'

The woman studied the gold cards and set them down. '*Liebling*, we can't – '

'Can't what?'

'It's impossible.'

'It's a present, like at Christmas. Only better.'

'It's not that – ' The woman started to cough again. She propped her head on an arm. There was sweat on her skin. 'We have no clothes, no shoes...'

'Your best dress!'

'At the Karntnerthor Theatre ladies wear silks and ribbons; their cloaks are of the finest cloth, they have shoes just for the evening...'

'That's not – '

'*Liebling*, it's in Vienna!'

'But – '

The woman pulled herself up.

'I will not be shamed –' She coughed, spat into the rag. 'I have lived with shame...' For all the coughing and the blood, the sentence will never be finished. Love protects. And love is here.

'There's money now – '

'We must be cautious.' The woman reached for her daughter, '*Liebling*, I'm sorry – '

'But I'll bring him luck. He said–'

A hand pushed the tickets forward. 'Take them back.

Present my compliments to your music man, thank him for his kindness, and say that, unfortunately, on that evening we have a prior engagement.'

'*Mutti*, please — '

'Do it now.'

•   •   •

Heavy-footed, the child moved along the streets, the tickets smouldering like live coals in her hand. Had she looked up she would have observed that here and there, things that grew in parks and in gardens were in bud.

It was spring.

Sixteen

She lurched on. She heard her name called, heard those seductive sounds she knew so well. She kept her head down and measured her way in cobblestones.

The man wasn't there. The door to the house in the Reinerstrasse was locked. She peered through the window – everything was as it had been...

What to do?

The tickets would fit beneath the door but leaving them would be wrong. He would think, now not every seat will be filled. And his fear would grow...

There was only one thing to do. Wait.

She sat on the step. She studied the cards in her hand, traced the shapes of words until they blurred and were lost to sight. With her knees clasped to her chest she rocked back and forth, and back and forth; and the rhythm was that of the song of joy...

Long she remained until the rooftops and the chimneys had locked out the sun. Then she started for home.

Seventeen

In the house by the granary a light was glowing and as she opened the door she heard a voice. That of Frau Schwarz.

The child halted, considered the conifer, the berry bush, other places of concealment.

'Is that you, *Liebling?*'

'Yes, *Mutti.*'

Frau Schwarz was large and loud. She listened at keyholes. Frau Schwarz knew what was going on. She was also kind, and broth and meat stew and sometimes an orange cake would appear on a doorstep. 'Such a load of nonsense,' was a favourite of Frau Schwarz.

'*Guten Tag* Frau Schwarz.' The child turned to her mother. 'He wasn't there.'

'Who wasn't there?'

The woman was coughing again. 'No-one to speak of, Frau Schwarz.'

Eyes switched from mother to daughter, 'What's going on, Child? You look unhappy.'

'We were given tickets to a concert — show our guest, *Liebling*.'

The guest reached for her spectacles. She read, she looked up. 'These are for the Karntnerthor Theatre!'

'They were a gift.'

'From whom?'

'A friend. His new work is being performed.'

'I know nothing of music —' began Frau Schwarz.

'Nor I.'

'— But I know the value of these . . .'

The woman stared down, squeezed tight the rag. 'We are not going,' she said.

'Why ever not?'

'We are otherwise engaged.' It was the child who spoke.

'Such a load of nonsense!'

'We could go,' her mother continued, 'but other things are more important.'

Frau Schwarz peered at the speaker. 'Such a load of nonsense, it's just what you need. Put colour in your cheeks. Take your mind off "other things".'

'We've given the tickets back and that's an end to it.'

'They're here, on the table.' The speaker fixed her eyes on the child. 'What's going on?'

The child dropped her head.

'You want to go, don't you? I can see that you do. Answer me, Child.' Frau Schwarz leaned close, held the pause, 'But you have a problem. You need a dress. A beautiful gown of pink . . .'

'No, blue.'

Nobody spoke.

'At a certain factory there is a box,' Frau Schwarz began. 'In it are lengths of silk long enough for a dress – for two dresses...'

'Frau Schwarz, please – '

'Herr Rohrmann, who dyes cloth, is a friend, Frau Praetz, the purveyor of ribbons, also, and were you aware that your neighbour has donated a bolt of her exquisite lace to the Guild – of which I am the president – for a "variety of purposes"?'

'Frau Schwarz – '

'– These are good people...' The voice dropped. 'Do it for the child – ' The speaker eased back in her chair, she wiped her brow. 'Not going? Such a load of nonsense!'

'*Mutti*?'

The woman sat at the table and held her tears.

'Please...'

A head nodded.

The child lunged, was lost in folds of flesh, '*Danke*, Frau Schwarz, *Danke, Danke, Danke*...'

'Goodness, Child – ' Frau Schwarz blushed rose colour and fumbled for her spectacles... 'Such a load of nonsense!... Now listen to me carefully. On Monday I shall go to the factory and you will accompany me...'

The women talked on...To the child it was like the sounds the man made on the piano when one hand spoke to the other...

'Two weeks is short.'

'We work at night.'

'And who are "we"?'

'Just you and me.'

'Our boots –?'

'Will be covered.'

'Our hair?'

'Will be curled.'

'If I cough.'

'There are lozenges.'

'And how do we get there?'

The rhythm changed. 'Child, run and fetch *Mutti's* sewing box.'

'Why are you doing this, Frau Schwarz?' the woman asked.

'I don't like things to beat me.'

'That's not all, is it?'

'No, that's not all ... ah, thank you, Child. Now to take measurements. Both of you – up!'

Eighteen

They got to the factory as a wave of women began to surge towards the gate.

'Pardon me, ladies – '

The women paused, turned to the speaker, a few edged closer.

'A word if you please. I don't speak for myself but for this dear child – '

They were listening.

The voice set the scene. Went on. 'I know of the box and that in it is silk with small flaws, but enough for – '

There was stirring. Women glanced at each other. Some moved off.

'That's for cushions, lady.'

'And linings.'

More moved away.

'Ladies, you haven't heard this simple request – '

'If it's that simple, you do it!'

'I'm sorry,' someone in a green kerchief mumbled. And hurried off.

'Well!' exclaimed Frau Schwarz. She squared her shoulders, straightened her spectacles and turned to face the second wave of workers. 'Let's hope this lot are more amenable,' she muttered.

The second wave simply pushed past.

'I expect they're tired.' Frau Schwarz smiled. But behind the spectacles, eyes glinted.

'These must be the last,' she announced as about forty women in twos and threes started to straggle out.

'Pardon me, ladies – ' Again she began, but this time all were 'sisters-in-arms'. 'Such an opportunity – one each of us would remember forever...' Frau Schwarz was struggling. 'All I ask – not for myself – is two lengths, flawed though they be and of little value...' A pause to dab at cheeks, lips. 'Who will be kind enough, generous enough to perform this simple task?'

'Not me, lady.'

'Nor me.'

'Me neither.'

'I will!'

There was a hush. Eyes turned and followed the speaker as she pushed to the front. A small fair-haired woman stood before Frau Schwarz. 'I will,' she repeated. 'Advise me of the lengths and an address and I will see that they are delivered.'

Bodies inched forward. There was shuffling, muttering...

'She's mad – '

'She'll lose her place — '

The woman spoke. 'My man was killed. I was despairing ... I was alone and without hope. Then a child showed me a kindness. It was a simple gesture but it gave me strength ... This is the child ... '

·   ·   ·

'Well!'

They waited on a street corner.

'Well, well!' uttered Frau Schwarz yet again and waved down a carriage. With a flick of a whip the horse clopped on.

Frau Schwarz studied flaxen braids that fell across a bib. 'What is it, Child? Look at me.'

The child raised her head.

'It's that woman, isn't it? You're worried that she will lose her place in embroidery because of this. Such a load of nonsense! I assure you, she will not regret what she has done. She will always have her place. Always. I give you my word. You understand me?'

The child nodded. She suddenly remembered a tale that had been told to them in class. It was of the good witch of Korneuburg, whose wondrous powers changed lives. 'The good witch,' her teacher had said, 'was a giant among mortals ...' The child studied Frau Schwarz in her largeness. And wondered.

Nineteen

The following week brought Frau Schwarz with her
sewing box and a letter.

Now, when lessons were over the child would reach
for her satchel and run. But not in the direction of the
Reinerstrasse. Others noticed, made questioning gestures,
appointed this one and that to follow and report. But where
once they had ridiculed the stumbling on cobblestones, now
they saw sprinting and skipping. Even the mother whom
she met was brighter in her step. And livelier too.

The watchers kicked at stones. And said nothing.

What they didn't know was that in the house by
the granary, silk and lace and lengths of ribbon were
being transformed into gowns of cream and blue that
Cinderella herself might have worn to the ball...

At the kitchen table the child sat ready to pass pins,
thread needles, trace patterns, and make coffee, while her
mother and Frau Schwarz measured and cut and stitched
and tucked. From time to time the woman would cough,
spit into a rag and work on...

And the day passed and became the next day and with it came a letter.

'From Papa.' The woman announced. She read, folded the pages and said nothing.

'Is it Fritz?'

'Who?'

'The squirrel.'

'No.'

'What then?'

'The rash. He had to report it.'

'You said not to.'

'He's been given a liniment to rub on.'

The child loves her papa but she cannot focus on liniment and legs. She cannot think of anything but a man, and a sound, and a dress of blue silk . . .

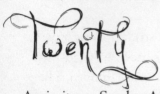

Twenty

Again it was Sunday. And in four more days (ninety-six hours minus three, to be precise) then . . .

She had waited on the step of the house in the Reinerstrasse for three days now but the door had remained locked.

And again it was Sunday. And again the man was not there. And in the house by the granary a dress of blue silk floated like gossamer from its peg.

The child wandered in silence and within herself. Oblivious to the colours and shapes that formed and reformed, kaleidoscope-like, as through the early morning she moved.

At the edge of the town where the river runs she halted. She entered the Vienna Woods. How long it had been since she'd climbed into the tree, she couldn't measure, though the maples, the beeches, the oaks and the elms had turned a million shades of green. And, like paint when it's splashed upon a canvas, so wild flowers, snowdrops, cyclamens and lilies of the valley splashed the earth with their colour.

And people in the colours of the flowers came. They strolled along paths, talking and laughing – and silently too.

Huddled tight between new leaves the child dreamed. She dreamed of a castle as Rauhenstein was long ago, and of a princess with golden hair who had been held captive there and who wore a blue dress ...

Then she saw him. The man was striding along a path, his head down, his hands behind his back. As he got to where the path swung towards the tree, she jumped. The man stopped. He opened his mouth as though to speak, but instead just shook his head and moved on. The child followed.

Something had happened. Something terrible. It was in the eyes, the jutting lip ...

The man strode, stopped, sat, strode again. He made no sound. The child clutched at her pinafore. The bib had been ripped as she'd jumped, though she'd heard nothing.

Again he sat. This time he didn't move on. At his feet, snowdrops and wild violets grew. Long he stared as though he would paint them, then he raised his eyes. The child had seen the same look in the eyes of her father. It was the look of fear ... She stood silent. Even with the conversation book and a scribe by her side, she wouldn't have been able to frame the words.

She couldn't speak.

He couldn't hear.

She stood, silent among the snowdrops, and clutched her torn bib.

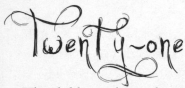

Twenty-one

The child stared into the night. A highwayman's moon
cast its dappled light on rose bush and rooftop, on the
outstretched arms of an apple tree in bloom. Dappled
light on whitewashed walls formed and faded in markings
that made music. If she could read them they would
sing...

She curled onto her bed and pulled the coverlet up.
Now she would pray. She'd seen it done. She closed her
eyes, squeezed tight her hands and began...

'Please God, help him. He's frightened they'll laugh
like they did before and no-one will come. And if you
could hear it, you'd think it was so beautiful ... Please
God, please make them come and not laugh...

'*Auf Wiedersehen* – and thank you for listening ...'

Twenty-two

'*Mutti!*'

Two letters in one week! The woman frowned and slipped it into her bodice as the child entered.

'Can we try our dress on?'

'Our dress?'

'Yours too. Pleeeeease?'

The woman took the gowns from their pegs. She held hers to her body. Frau Schwarz was right, cream silk against primrose lace did make her cheeks glow.

'You're beautiful,' said the child.

'So are you, *Liebling*.'

They giggled. They glided like swans. They waltzed across the floor. Princesses on stone...

'*Mutti*, you've dropped a letter.'

'It's from Papa.'

The child continued to waltz. 'Did you tell him?'

'What?'

'About the dress?'

'Papa is proud,' the woman answered. In her hand

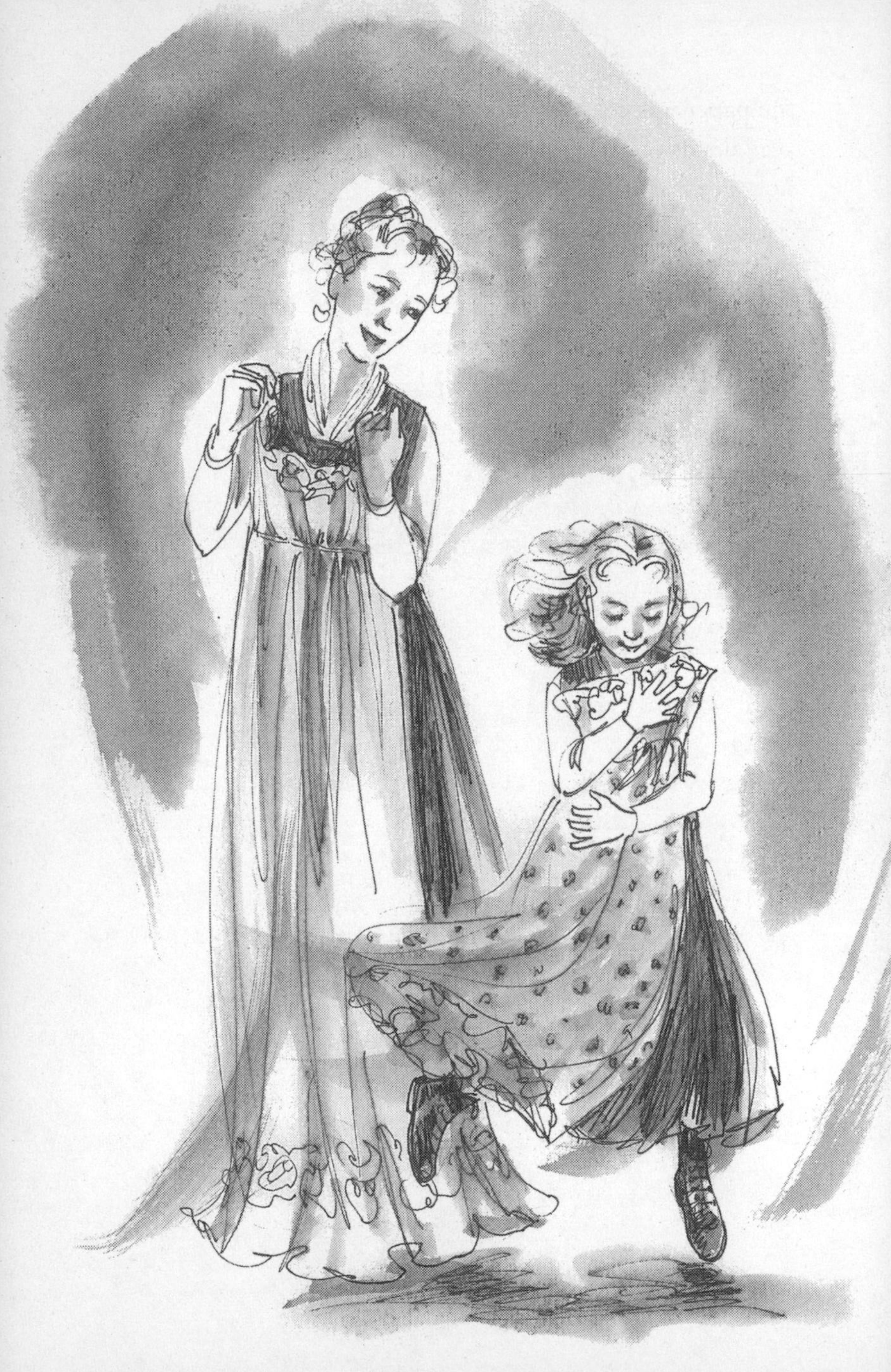

the paper was cold. Cold, and as bleak as the message it contained would most certainly be. She would read it but not speak of it.

The child danced on. Everything would be all right. God was all seeing and all powerful. Her teacher said...

'I'll make a picture for Frau Schwarz of us dancing,' she chirruped. 'And one for Papa too...'

She went in search of paper and crayons...

Twenty-Three

At the house in the Reinerstrasse the man was writing. An empty flask rocked to and fro along the floor. The night was wild, and papers fluttered in a draught of wind.

It was a frenzy of writing...

'...as I reflect upon my miserable life,' he wrote, 'I am God's unhappiest creature. Not to hear... If I belonged to any other profession, it would not be quite so bad; but in my profession this is a terrible affliction... All hope of being cured has faded like the fallen leaves of autumn... As for my music I am filled with dread...'

The pen fell from his hand. The darkness deepened. Suddenly he sat up. Something was different. It was the light. He pulled back the curtains and opened the window. It was snowing. Sheets of snow fell from the trees and the rooftops, and on the ground, carriages and carts ploughed furrows deep as trenches.

He heard the town hall clock strike midnight, and as

it did, a phantom-like creature in a black cloak appeared beneath his window and beckoned to him...

The man stepped from the door. It was cold. His boots sank in the snow, but the hand kept urging him on. Everywhere there were people, lots of people, stamping their feet and beating their hands on their chests in an effort to keep warm... He moved on, keeping the black cloak in sight. From time to time he stumbled in a drift of snow.

The strange creature had turned into a building, a place so derelict it was falling down; its beams splayed like fingers against the sky.

The man followed. Along corridors through which snowflakes circled he went. At a door that hung from one hinge the creature stopped. He pushed against it.

The room was big. From broken beams and gaping glass snowflakes swirled, they filled each crevice and corner.

In the room there were chairs, hundreds and hundreds of empty chairs, and gathered together, grumbling and mumbling, was a crowd of phantom-like creatures similar to the first, in black cloaks.

As the man stood there, two of them started to sing but since they couldn't be heard above the mumbling and grumbling they began to sing louder and louder. They raised their voices and bellowed like bulls. The man put his hands to his ears, for strangely he could hear everything.

When he looked up the hand was beckoning again. He moved forward, and as he did the black cloaks parted to reveal what looked like a piano. It was exactly like a piano but it had no keys. The man recoiled in terror, for now all the people who had been in the snow had gathered in the room and were chanting 'Play, play, play . . . Play, play, play . . .'

'I can't.'

'Play, play, play . . .'

'There are no keys — '

One started to laugh, and then another and another and now the whole room was rocking with laughter. Laughter, loud and terrible . . .

•   •   •

The man blinked, he opened his eyes. He was in his bed. He was in his clothes, but this was his bed. There was sweat in his eyes and on his hands . . . He staggered up, shuffled through food and paper and clothes . . .

He flung open the window and looked out upon the morning with its soft murmurings of spring . . .

Twenty-four

The days yawn, the nights stretch sleepless, one after the other... And a child counts the hours and the minutes and dreams of a tomorrow.

And now the day before tomorrow had come.

In the kitchen in her silk dress with blue lace and blue ribbons, the child practised walking. She had perfected a way to move so as to conceal all but the very tips of her newly covered boots. Around the table she glided, her shadow shape recurring on woodwork and glass...

As the sun slipped behind the granary Frau Schwarz arrived with a hessian bag, curling irons and a guessing game.

The child sat very still, she watched transfixed as her hair turned from heavy braids to the waving locks of the princess in her story book. She thought, now I know why people who are beautiful are smiling inside, like my mother is now... And the woman caught her daughter's look and knew her thinking... She smiled back. A smile that said this is not us, we're simply Cinderella having her moment at the ball. But in having it, the memory will be there always and forever ... She stretched wide her arms and held her daughter close ...

Frau Schwarz took off her spectacles and dabbed her eyes. Her nose also.

'Frau Schwarz is our fairy godmother,' declared the child.

'Such a load of nonsense.' The guest fumbled for her handkerchief and blew loudly. 'Well, Child – ' She pointed to the bag. 'As you gather, I have been to market. Tell me, what do you see on top of these parcels?'

'A pumpkin.'

'Is it?'

'Yes.'

Frau Schwarz mused, went hum and hah. 'What if I said it was not a pumpkin but something else?'

The child was silent.

'Can you guess?'

'No, Frau Schwarz.'

'Well, think about it. I will come tomorrow for your answer.'

The child turned to her mother who was most certainly hiding a smile ...

Twenty-Five

Tomorrow comes.

The child cannot concentrate. The teacher speaks words she does not hear. The dots and dashes on the blackboard she does not see. She raises her hand because everybody else is ... She watches the hands on the round-faced clock measuring time in slow time ...

The day will never end ...

. . .

On the table were bowls of broth and newly baked bread.

'I can't – '

'You must eat,' her mother replied.

In silence, mother and daughter drank broth ...

As the dishes were being packed away Frau Schwarz strode in, first to compliment the weather, then, 'Have you thought of an answer, Child?'

'No, Frau Schwarz.'

'Go to the window.'

The child crossed the room ...

'What do you see?'

In the street stood an old four-wheeled, wide-hooded landau.

'A carriage,' the child replied.

'Are you certain?'

'Yes.'

'That's a relief. It was a pumpkin a moment ago.'

The child gaped. The woman laughed. The guest feigned surprise. 'To drive through Vienna in a pumpkin would be strange, don't you agree? And now, the hair and then to dress...'

In a blue dress with her braids falling free, the child watched for her mother. She appeared, a vision in cream, side curls framing her face...

'Time,' announced Frau Schwarz.

As in all the best fairytales, the carriage rolled away, if not into the sunset, then along streets splashed with late afternoon light. Down unknown and familiar paths the horse clopped. On and on, past the council buildings and into the Kaiserstrasse where the child had sat with her father and heard the street musicians play. The woman peered into the fast closing day. This was exciting. She pointed out new buildings, monuments and parklands. The child was silent. This was to be her moment of joy, this was what she had waited for, counted the hours and the minutes for. And now all she felt was fear...

Darkness fell. And still into the moving night they drove...

The driver flicked the whip. The horse turned a corner. And before them shone the lights of Vienna.

The horse turned again, this time into a street of elms. And there it was.

Both stared.

It was indeed like a scene from a fairytale in which beautiful women in silks and laces, with glittering shoes and ribbons and feathers, stepped from carriages on the arms of equally beautiful men in black and white, with silk hats, and all of them were talking and laughing and waving to each other and pushing forward. As one they moved towards the arched door of a magnificent building whose sculpted edifice rose against the sky.

The Karntnerthor Theatre.

Mother and daughter stepped down also. They stood apart as the driver joined the queue of carriages that were lined up. Silk pressed against silk and feathers tickled as they entered the theatre.

Through rose light and mirrors they shuffled to where gowns and suits were lining up to present their tickets and take their seats.

They joined the queue, and moved in ...

Neither spoke. This was far beyond a dream. There were no words for this. They followed an usher down the aisle in the direction of the stage; down and down the red carpet they went, right to row four. They stared at the seats, at each other. They sat, the child on the aisle.

In front of them was the stage with its curtain of velvet. They tried to take in the mouldings, the engravings in gold leaf, the marble statues, the richly painted frescoes, the scalloped drapes . . . the boxes, also carved in gold leaf, that rose at the sides and beyond the boxes, again, embossed in gold, the galleries – the child counted one two three four – five levels . . . And towering above, the sculpted dome, from which three enormous chandeliers dropped on heavy chains . . .

The whole place glowed.

The child swung around. Behind her stretched row after row after row into which people were streaming.

There would be no empty seat.

She turned back to the stage. A huge stage and deserted but for drums and double basses, seats and music stands . . .

The child listened. The sound was like the buzzing of giant flies . . .

The buzzing grew louder, for now the musicians had entered. Men in evening dress were filling up the stage, moving to their seats, sitting, talking to each other, making strange sounds on their instruments . . .

Next the choir filed in. Here there were women as well. And now two other men took their seats at the front and two women, one in gold and the other in blue, took theirs.

'The soloists,' her mother whispered.

The buzzing was fading, stuttering like flies when they die . . . to nothing. To silence . . .

The child was finding it hard to breathe. She closed her eyes. She put her hands to her ears. She talked to God...

And now came clapping for Kapellmeister Umlauf was walking across the stage, and the man with him.

The conductor stepped onto the podium, turned to the audience and bowed. The man stood at the far side and faced the players. He did look splendid, though smaller and somehow unimportant, like the toy in the nursery that's discarded. The child breathed deeper, harder.

A hush louder than any silence descended as Kapellmeister Umlauf turned to the orchestra and raised his baton. The child sat forward, her heart ready to fly, to soar with the music...

It started slowly, the strings and the horns sang of loss, of empty nothingness... Sounds the child hadn't heard before but as she listened, the sounds became stronger and stronger and louder and louder, they were building into a wild and terrible storm, as the drums rolled like thunder and the strings flashed like lightning across the sky...

And all the while the man stood facing the players and waved his baton back and forth... And heard nothing...

The music changed. Now the child saw dancing. People in a circle passed lengths of flowers to each other as they went twisting and turning in and around...

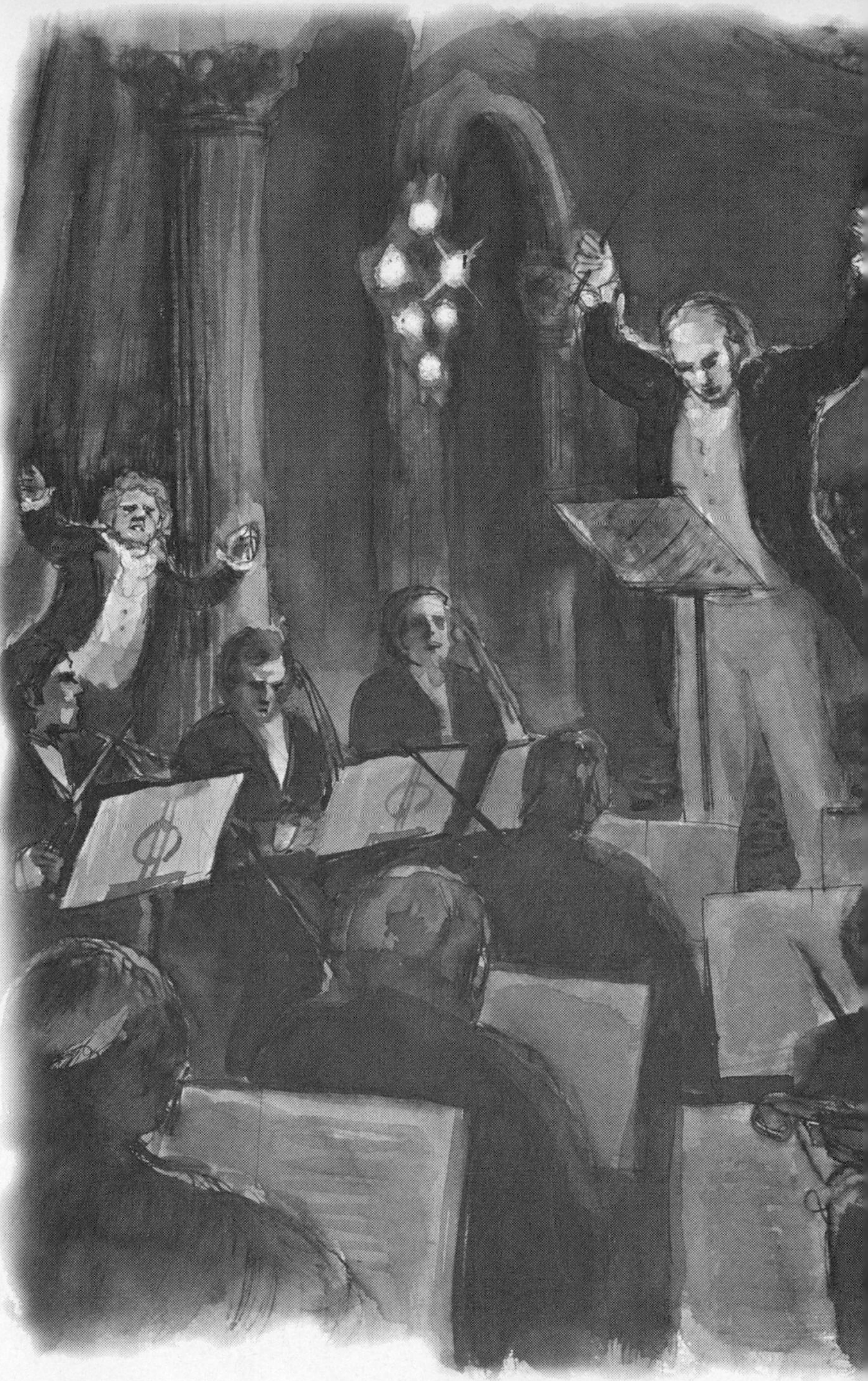

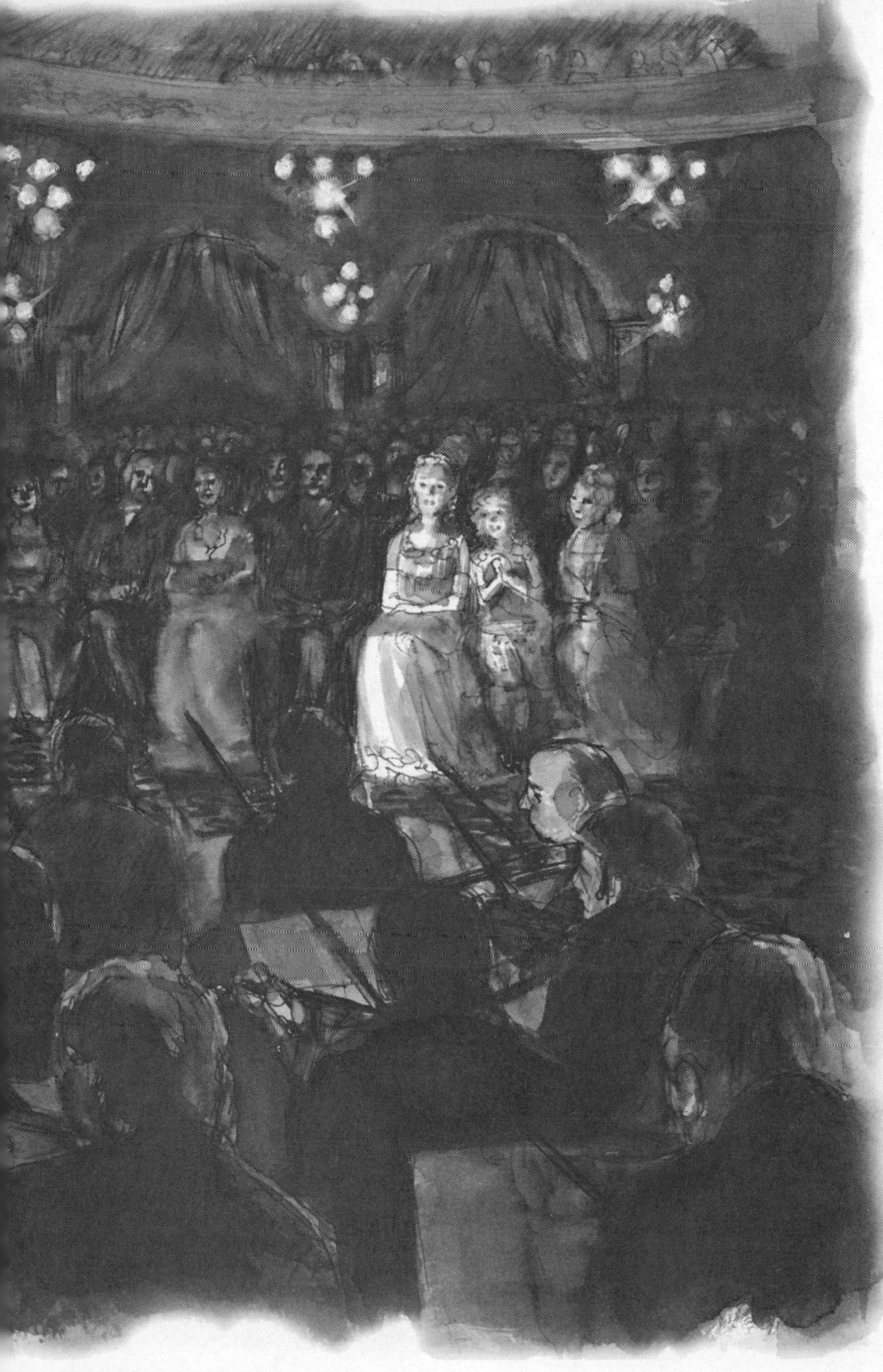

Again the sound changed. This time the strings were singing of a great beauty like the russet glow of autumn that speaks of death. A sob rose in her throat. She turned to her mother who was weeping too . . .

And then it came.

The sound burst open and every instrument with it, and a choir of angels extolled it and the 'Ode to Joy' exploded into a million voices and every heart sang at the promise of peace and love and happiness and hope and all that ever and ever was rich and wonderful . . . And the child looked, and saw the roof beams quiver. And she knew without thought that she would never be lonely again . . .

And the strings were rising, and rising, they rose to the most jubilant eruption of sound that ever was heard . . .

It was over.

There was silence. No movement. Nothing.

Then suddenly there came a volley of sound, for the whole audience had jumped to its feet and were clapping and cheering and shouting and throwing their hats in the air and waving their handkerchiefs . . . and going mad . . .

'Turn around, turn around,' whispered the child.

On the podium Kapellmeister Umlauf was bowing. He bowed again. Again and again he bowed. But the man didn't move.

'Turn around, turn around,' whispered the child.

The clapping and cheering, the shouting and waving was getting louder, wilder . . .

Still the man didn't turn...

The child slipped from her seat: quick like a mouse she was at the stage and tugging a trouser leg.

He looked down.

He turned.

It was only then that he realised that he had written something of unparalleled mastery.

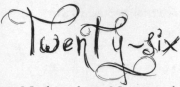

Twenty-six

Nothing lasts. Not even the most perfect moment ... It can only be relived in memory.

This the child is doing over and over, as in the darkness of early morning she steps from the carriage. As she enters the house she murmurs a silent thanks ...

In the kitchen she takes down a glass and reaches for water ...

The next day the heat's inside her skin.

• • •

'It's a fever.'

'I'm just hot.'

'It's a fever,' repeated the woman. 'Into bed.'

The child lay on her bed. Her head throbbed. The light hurt. Her mother sponged her face and arms. 'Too much excitement,' she said. She dispensed liquids and read stories ...

The child slept through the night and through the next day and the next and when she awoke she was grumpy.

'You're getting better,' her mother remarked. They sat

at the table and drank broth. 'Can I go for a walk?' asked the child.

'Tomorrow – maybe.'

Now she was feeling well, the child noticed things. The rag her mother used for the cough was now permanently inside the bodice of her dress. And there was something else.

'Is Papa sick?'

'No, *Liebling*.'

'Then –?'

The woman coughed hard, held the rag to her face. 'In two days, if you're quite well we'll both go back... All will be right, *Liebling*... '

But something wasn't. The child could tell...

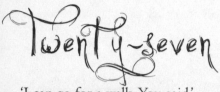

Twenty-seven

'I can go for a walk. You said.'

The woman made a fist, pressed cheeks, a brow, and nodded. 'The fresh air will do you good. Wear your coat and go slowly.'

The day was pink, the air warm against skin. In the sky rode puffs of coppery cloud. The child wanted to run but went slowly as her mother said...

Music was coming from the house in the Reinerstrasse. She stood at the door.

The man played a series of rollicking chords and came towards her. 'At last, here she is, looking like a woolly bear. Are you sick? Were you sick? I say to myself, *meine kleine Blume* is hiding away, she thinks there is no joy in my music. That I am the most ridiculous of musicians. Am I right?'

The child shook her head.

'So, did she like it?'

A frantic nodding of head.

'Am I not a genius? Am I not brilliant like the stars?'

'Yes!'

'In that case you must know the answer. What was it you saw in the music, little flower. Write it.'

The child went to the small table, wrote 'STORM.'

'Yes.'

'DANCE.'

'Yes.'

'TEARS.'

'Yes – and the last?'

She dropped the pencil and jumped up; she stood on tip-toe, threw back her head, her arms wide.

The man was silent. 'How strange . . .' he murmured. 'She knows what others older and wiser have no comprehension of – it is a mystery, this feeling for music that is instinctive in a child.' He moved closer. His teeth were yellow, his skin gnarled and peeling like an old tree. 'I felt your presence there in the fourth row, it gave me comfort.' He looked hard and long into the child. 'There is trust in those blue eyes and pain too . . . You speak without words . . . Words are such an impediment to feeling . . . Music is the only truth . . .' He broke into a laugh. 'Did you see the roof beams tremble?'

'Yes.'

'Was it not magnificent!'

'Yes.'

'Da dada dada dada dadada da dada . . .' And the man sang and the child sang . . . And a fist started banging on the door . . .

'Herr Umlauf, to tell me again how brilliant I am.'

The child slipped on her coat.

'We shall go to the woods and look for dragons and eat snowdrops, and dance among the lilies, yes?'

'Yes!'

. . .

At the gate her mother was waiting. She ran to her daughter and clutched her hard. '*Liebling*, I have wonderful news. Wonderful, wonderful news – ' She started to cough and felt for the rag. Her cheeks were pink, unnaturally so . . .

'What?'

'Papa is coming home!'

'Papa, home?'

'Is this not happy news?'

'Yes!'

The woman sat at the table, her head in her hands, 'I've been so worried. I thought . . . But he has left the army for something better – something much better.' She pulled herself up, took the child's hand. 'You see, he has a friend – '

'Fritz.'

'Manfred. And Manfred's papa is a farrier, a blacksmith, like our papa, but Manfred's papa is old and is wanting someone to work in his forge, and to be in charge of it too . . . This work is exactly what papa loves . . . And there's more. With the forge comes a house! Yes! Manfred's papa is to live with his daughter . . . '

'Oh, *Mutti!*'

'I knew my *Liebling* would be happy ...'

'When?'

'I am packing already.'

In her trundle bed the child traced patterns of moonlight and dreamed. Life was beautiful. She was the happiest, the luckiest, the bluest of the most beautiful little blue flowers that ever grew – and her papa was coming home.

This would change everything...

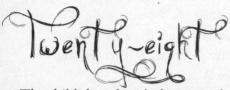

Twenty-eight

The child thought, it's the music that has brought him back. I sent the sounds of joy from my head to his and he heard and he's coming home ... The teacher tapped with her ruler and frowned. The child worked on, the letters and numbers far from her thoughts ...

The man was not at the house in the Reinerstrasse that afternoon. Nor was he there the next, or the next ...

Where was he? Thinking aloud, the child made her way to the factory gate.

'She's gone,' a woman remarked.

By the giant conifer beyond her window, her mother was waiting. 'I've got a surprise,' she said.

'Papa!' The child leapt, was gathered into strong arms.

A hand stroked her head. 'Your papa has come home to his sweet girl – is she not happy?'

'Yes.'

'We shall be a family again, the three of us. What fun we'll have ... We'll go fishing and picnicking – and sing loudly in the street ...'

'Papa!'

'We can, *Liebling*. The forge is far from the town square. It's where the factories are and a certain cafe that makes very excellent coffee, I hear – '

'But – '

'Is it not wonderful, *Liebling*?'

'Is *Mutti's* factory near?'

'Goodness me, no. *Mutti's* factory is here. Did she not tell you? We are going to Wiener Neustadt – '

'What?'

'It's a whole day's journey from here.'

'We're going away?'

'Yes!'

'Leaving Baden?'

'Didn't *Mutti* talk about the house? *Liebling*, it is big. You will have your own room. Think of that!'

Silence.

'And better than anything – *Mutti* will not be working ... Not in any factory.'

'No – '

'Yes. There is only one forge in the town and there is much work – '

'No – NO ...'

The man paused. 'Forgive me, *Liebling*, I know this is a shock for you. But a change will be good for all of us.' He lifted a box from the floor. 'We must help *Mutti* pack,' he said.

The child grabbed his arm. 'When?'

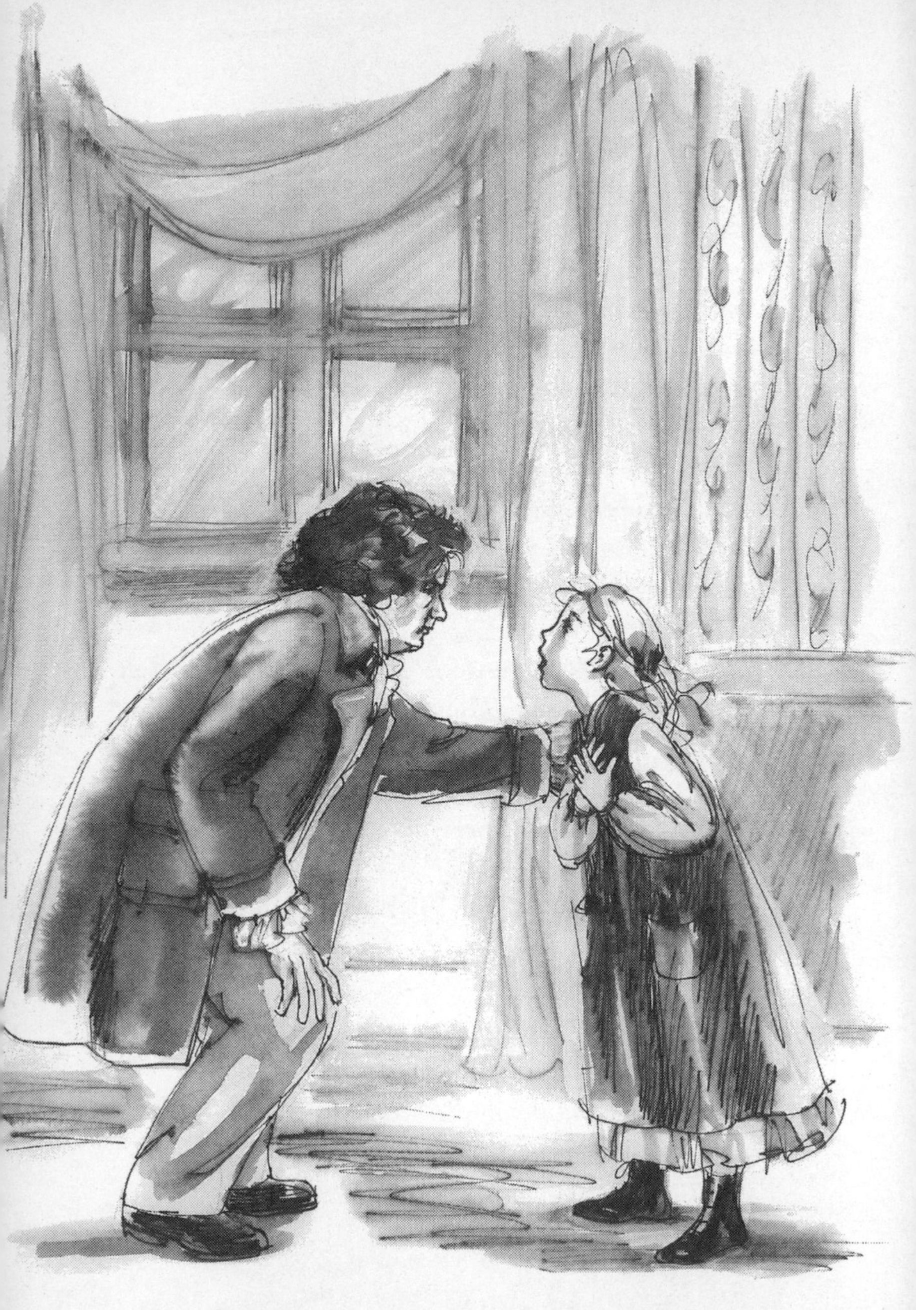

'Soon.'

'What's soon?'

'The cart will be here at five. We will travel at night.'

'What day –?'

'Today.'

Statue-like the child stood, and stared into nothing.

'You are worried that you are leaving your friends.
I understand, but everything has happened so fast and one
cannot leave a forge idle...'

The child made a rush for the door.

'Of course, you wish to say farewell. But hurry – we
leave at five.'

Into the setting sun she ran. Into the wind that
whipped trees and flowers, that tossed leaves and papers
into the air...A ribbon on a braid fell free and skeins of
hair slashed her face and into her eyes. She ran, she pushed
past workers holding their hats, past woman with shopping
bags...Panting and gasping, she entered the Reinerstrasse.
What if he's not there? He wasn't yesterday or the day
before...Please God let him be there...Please...Please...

The man was there.

The child held her head in her hands, her chest was
heaving, she didn't – couldn't speak...

'What has happened?' he asked.

'Leaving,' she mouthed...

'Leaving what?'

She dropped her head.

'The town?'

She nodded.

'Your *Vater* – he is no longer with the army?'

She nodded.

'He has a position, where?'

The child staggered to the small table. Wrote 'Wiener Neustadt'.

'I see. And you have come to tell me this. And when are you leaving? In a month? A week? Tomorrow? ... Now?'

'Yes.'

'Ah –'

'I don't want to ... I don't want to go ... be away from you ... from the music ...' The pencil dropped to the floor.

The man smiled, a smile that was both tender and sad. 'No-one has ever wept for me – ' he murmured. He took the child by the hand. 'Bless you for that. Now, dry your eyes, you don't want your papa to see tears – '

The child took the handkerchief, ran a hand over her eyes, stumbled towards the door ...

'Wait!'

She stopped.

'Write your name.'

She picked up the pencil and wrote. Again she moved to the door. '*Auf Wiedersehen*,' she whispered.

Along the street she rushed, then stopped. Once more she had heard his voice. 'God keep you, Little One,' he called.

From the house in the Reinerstrasse for the last time,

she ran. Still sobbing, she entered the marketplace. She leaned against the trunk of a tree until her breathing steadied.

She was only a child, yet she was learning the greatest of all life's wisdoms. That it is not pain, or even cruelty that makes a heart break. It is love.

Outside the house in the street by the granary, the cart was waiting . . .

PART 2

The Worker on the Factory Floor

One

In Wiener Neustadt the day was coming to an end.

At a factory in the industrial part of the town the
gates had opened and the workers were tumbling out.
Trailing behind them were two girls of about fourteen.
They ambled across the yard and into the street.

One was dark and one was fair and each wore her hair
with side curls, as was the fashion...

They came to a corner, waved their goodbyes and went
their own ways.

The fair girl crossed the street and proceeded to cut
through a field. Here and there clusters of purple and
pink told of violets and cyclamens. She bent to pick some,
choosing only those perfect in size and shape; wound
them into a bunch and tied them together with a length
of wool.

It was spring. The time of rebirth, the most beautiful
of the seasons. She breathed its soft air and in an old
oak's trembling leaves, heard music that told of the joy
of it...

The field led to a graveyard. The girl pushed at the listing gate. She moved through waves of grass, past ancient and forgotten tombs, by angels with broken wings and empty urns, to where the new headstones stood.

At one she stopped. She brushed the stone free of dust and leaves and set down the blooms.

She stood quietly. She heard the sounds of silence; saw the spring colours glow in the evening sun. She lifted her fingers to her lips and placed a kiss on the warm stone.

This she did every day . . .

She moved away. Soon night would fall and her father would be hungry when he arrived home.

There was a time when he would have gone to the tavern. But that was in another place . . .

He didn't drink now. He rarely went out. Though sometimes in the evening he would join his new friends for a game of billiards . . .

Through straggling grass the girl walked, remembering . . .

Over three years had passed since she had sat at the back of a cart and watched her world disappear.

Though that world had not disappeared. The man in the Reinerstrasse had never left her, he and his music were still as much a part of her as her hand was, or her arm . . . Sometimes in the evening, as she sat with the darning, she'd hear his voice. She knew it was her imagination; but there were times when her needle would drop and she'd look up . . .

She never spoke of the man or his music, and when asked if she missed her home, she'd just smile and shake her head.

And then one day a most unexpected thing happened...

Two

The day began with rain.

The girl fell in with others hurrying across the yard. In the doorway stood Herr Giersch. '*Guten Tag*, my friends,' he beamed.

'*Guten Tag*, Herr Giersch.'

'A lovely day, is it not?'

All shook rain from their coats.

The girl made her way to level one. Here the master weavers worked. The men who handled the looms were indeed masters. It wasn't easy to control such fine threads; one needed strength to balance the loom or there'd be vibrations. Silk was a thing of beauty, it deserved to be treated with care . . .

One loom stood idle. The girl saw herself seated at it, a master weaver, watching the silk grow with the touch of a hand. She went on gathering threads.

On level two Rita was sweeping up. On level two the women who embroidered worked, while on level three, the silk was being turned into undergarments for the rich.

The girl joined her friend. Together they collected scraps, emptied bins and kept the floor free of things discarded or spilt.

Rita had come from Baden also. The two ate cake and ice-cream at the cafe on the corner, they played shuttlecock and went folk dancing in the square. Rita wanted to be a designer and have her gowns in shop windows.

It was when the day was drawing to a close that Herr Giersch made the announcement. With Herr Graf at his side he made his way to level one and called for silence.

Everybody turned. Herr Giersch was excited. He described an exhibition that was to be held in the designing and manufacture of silk; and went on to say that certain factories had been notified, and that this was one. 'Our good name has obviously travelled far and wide,' he crowed. 'However, sadly – ' Herr Giersch wiped his lips, 'we cannot invite everyone – '

'Good,' a voice murmured.

'The invitation is for floor workers only. The objective being to inspire the young to become designers and sewers of silk. The names of the three who will accompany me will be drawn from a hat . . . '

'I could see my cousins, Heidi and Bernd,' declared Rita as they started to pack up. And added, 'I wonder if the designs will be as good as mine.'

But the girl wasn't thinking of designs, or of Rita's cousins, or indeed of anyone . . . All she could think of was that three of them would be going to Baden.

And Baden was home . . .

Three

The farrier looked thoughtful, he puffed on his pipe. Earlier his daughter had burst into the house claiming she had news; very excited about it, she was. But he had replied, 'I am black with grime, and I smell of horses. First, a bath and some food, then we talk...'

Now he looked thoughtful and puffed on his pipe. 'I think you have not been happy here,' he said.

'That's not true —'

'I think it is perhaps better to be in a smaller town.'

'I am not unhappy, Papa. But it would be nice to see —' The girl hesitated.

'Of course. I am pleased for you, *Liebling*. Save your Kreutzers and present the expense for the journey to your papa...'

'There is no charge, and the coach will collect us and bring us home!'

The farrier knocked out his pipe. 'That your friend will accompany you is good,' he said.

By the fireplace father and daughter sat, and stared

into an empty grate. They heard the shutters rattle in the wind, and a night-bird call ...

'Your mother would have been proud.'

'Yes'

The farrier nodded. 'You miss her too,' he said.

* * *

In the still of the night the girl awoke. She would escape the designs and the garments and race to the house in the Reinerstrasse. Maybe she'd hear some new music, more happy even than the 'Ode to Joy', or more beautiful than the sounds of moonlight – if that were possible ...

In dreams she was already there ...

Four

Through the dark of early morning hooves pounded.

The third member, a girl called Liesel, was the first to fall asleep. She leaned further and further to the right until her head rested on the shoulder of Herr Giersch. The four sat facing each other in pairs; alternately sleeping and waking with the movement of the coach...

Past sculptures of trees, by shadowy buildings and farm houses the horses galloped. The coach rocking and rattling on the rough roads...

The hours passed.

At last the girl leaned out. She looked towards the east and glimpsed the white light of morning. She nudged Rita. Together they watched the day awake, saw its colours grow stronger, heard its orchestra tune up in the lowing of cattle, the barking of work dogs and the bleating of sheep.

A squadron of brightly coloured birds flew overhead, squawking. And in the distance rose the ruins of Rauhenstein.

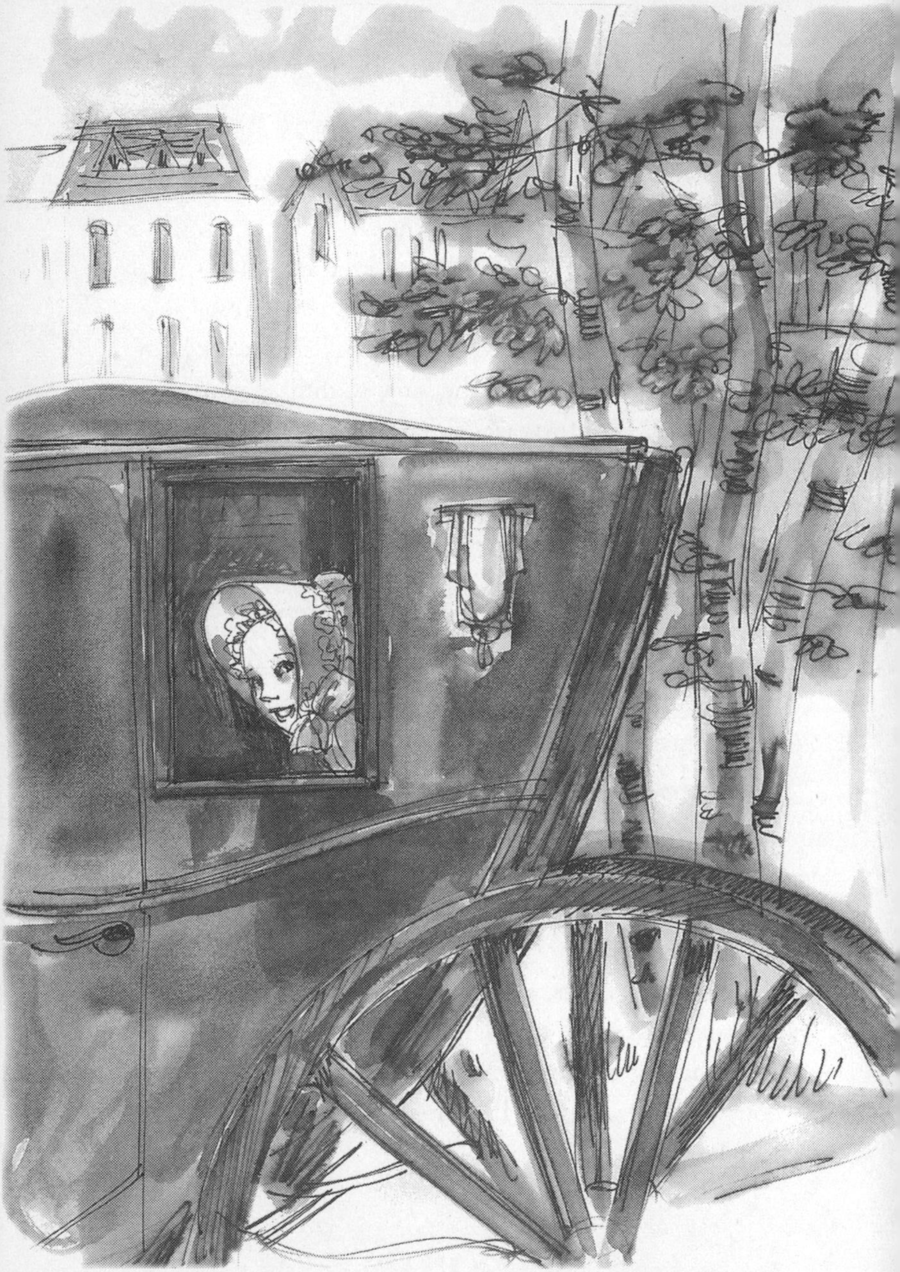

The girl turned to her friend with a smile that said, 'We're almost there.'

They were.

The horses pulled onto a grassy knoll near the square and stopped, snorting and panting.

The girl jumped down. She'd been fearful that things might have changed, but everything appeared to be as she remembered it. The town hall clock struck the hour in the same way and with the same sound as before. The column still stood with its shimmering star and cross of gold...

And it was market day. There was the same man in yellow, with his performing dogs; the same man played a waltz on the same squeaky fiddle. And the sounds joined with other sounds, as she had remembered them, with the calling of hawkers with their trays of trinkets and of vendors selling sausage and cheeses and fruit. And everywhere children ran with hoops and jumped like frogs on cobblestones...

'Over here,' called Rita.

They followed Herr Giersch into the town hall, where people were gathered around stands admiring the delicate chiffons and crepes, the array of designs and garments.

Together they moved between stands, keeping their eye not only on the wonders of silk but on Herr Giersch. They watched as a man in council regalia took him by the arm and led him away. They looked for Liesel...

'I'm going – '

'Me too,' said Rita.

The girl made her way through the square. As she went a young man caught her eye and winked. Something about him was familiar. Then suddenly she knew. He was one of the raggedy boys from the Volkschule who had made her life so unhappy. She couldn't help smiling...

She came to the Reinerstrasse and stopped. Her heart was thumping inside her chest.

The door to the house was locked and the curtains were closed. She examined each window and tried to peer inside. In one was a chink. She stood on tiptoe and looked in. Everything was as she pictured it, though perhaps the mess was more so. If she pressed her cheek to the glass she could see the edge of the piano...

She sat on the same step on which she had sat when she was nine, and waited. She smiled at the thought of seeing his expression when he discovered her there...

However, it seemed he wasn't coming.

She would return, there was time. Time, too, to visit the house by the granary.

She stood by the wooden gate, heard the rustle of needles in the conifer beyond which was once her window. Watched a cart carrying grain creak up the hill...

Down streets with elms in leaf she strolled. At the factory she halted; saw the door open and her mother run to her across the yard, her arms waving, her hair flying loose in the wind...

She wandered back through the now-empty square

to the fountain. Listened again to its whispering in the bubbling water. The water was cool and she drank deeply. It was a long walk to the home of Frau Schwarz.

As she set out she was surprised to see children in the streets. And as she turned a corner, a man with a black flag was walking in the centre of the road. He waved the flag above his head as he went.

She reached the house with the turret and knocked. She lingered in the garden, ran her hand over marble. Counted statues. Frau Schwarz was probably out helping someone . . .

The day edged on.

She returned to the Reinerstrasse. The door to the house was still locked.

The woods!

In the Vienna Woods the maples and the elms, the beeches and the oaks were once again heavy with leaf. Through snowdrops and violets she forced a path to her tree and climbed up.

Again she was nine. Now settled in the fork of its branches, she could hear the whispering of the day; in her mind's eye she saw carts trundling in and out of the marketplace, boys with hoops scooting behind wheels, wagons bearing families of picnickers, carriages winding along a forest drive . . .

Today the woods were deserted.

Down the empty path she watched for the strange figure with his shabby clothes and muddy boots that had walked towards her that first time, his long blue frockcoat billowing behind him, his hand attacking the air as he went.

She was just about to jump to the ground and return to his house when, like once before, she noticed something moving in the distance.

Again it was a funeral. This one was big. The carriage, draped in black, was drawn by four black horses. The coffin was covered with black cloth. Black plumes on the horses' heads bobbed and nodded as the procession started up the hill to the churchyard. Behind came people, hundreds of people, the line went on and on. It reached from the top of the hill to the bottom. And still they came...

She jumped down. She ran. In less than an hour she would be leaving.

Still the house in the Reinerstrasse remained locked. Again, on tiptoe, she peered through the chink in the curtain. Everything was as before.

She paced up and down the empty street. Where was he? Things happened to people. Her mother had done no wrong, yet... But he wrote music and music lives forever... He's giving another concert. He's written something new and again they're going on and on and he's going on and on...

Up and down and up and down...

The minutes remaining ticked by...

At the grassy knoll near the square the horses were

snorting and tossing their heads, impatient to leave. All three were there.

This was terrible, to be here and not to ...

Standing by the coach were Herr Giersch and the man from the council.

'My notebook,' she stammered. 'I left it.'

'Hurry. We leave in ten minutes.'

The door was still shut. She ripped a page from the notebook in her bag. 'I came – ' she scribbled. 'I – ' But there was neither time nor the words for it ... She crushed the paper in her fist ...

She drew her hand across her eyes in the same way she would when she was nine, and glanced for the last time along the street ...

ive

On a night blurred by rain, a coach drawn by four palominos drew up at an official building. The coachman sat on his box seat and waited.

A door opened and two men in livery and leather cockades stepped into the coach. With a tap on the roof from one, the coachman cracked his whip and they moved off.

Their mission was to reach the town of Wiener Neustadt by morning.

Into a night without stars the horses galloped.

Six

Morning had broken over Wiener Neustadt.

In the house by the forge the girl stirred. From her bed by the window she looked into faint patches of sun, the gentle light on grass and trees. She smelt the sweet scent of orange blossom and heard a bird warble its message from a rooftop . . .

She got up, peered along the end of the bed, then pulled the coverlet straight.

In the kitchen her father was drinking coffee. '*Guten Morgen, Liebling,*' he smiled.

'*Guten Morgen*, Papa.'

'I am sitting here wondering,' he went on, 'There is something I must see to, but what it is I do not know. My head is like a spinning top, so great is the order for hoes, irons, plough shares, and tools! The list to repair and make things goes on and on . . .'

'That is wonderful, Papa.'

'Like the little birds I must start early.'

'There is ham for your lunch. And cheese.'

'You spoil me, *Liebling*.' The farrier rose. He kissed his daughter and walked into the day.

The girl washed, dressed, tidied the kitchen and pulled the door closed.

The morning was pink and still. The sky was stippled with silvery cloud and the orange trees were white with blossom. As she moved through the grove a light wind rippled and a drift of petals, like snow, fell on her path, her hand, her hair ... And in the wind she heard the hymn of thanksgiving sung by the shepherd to his God after the storm had passed.

His sound. *His* voice saying, 'Music is the only truth.' She hadn't understood. And though she didn't still, her heart told her it was true.

If only she could turn back time, like you can a clock, or the pages of a book. To be nine again and to hear that voice and the magic of that music and feel again her heart about to burst with the joy of it; and to have her mother wave her hand as she crossed the yard, and turn the moment to gold ...

·   ·   ·

She flicked tears from her cheeks.

Mutti had said it was bad luck to cry on such a day ...

Rita was walking towards her, sniffing the air. 'It's wicked to be locked away on a day this beautiful ... '

'It's my birthday,' said the girl.

'Why didn't you tell me? I would have got you

something. Still – ' Rita glanced left and right, she leaned over a garden wall and plucked a rose. 'Happy birthday.'

'*Danke.*'

'And what did you get?'

'Papa knew there was something he had to remember – '

'If you'd told me I would have reminded him.'

'He loves me,' replied the girl. 'It's not important.' She stopped, then went on. 'Though I still checked the end of the bed. There'd always be something there on my birthday. *Mutti* would wrap it in paper and tie it with a ribbon ... '

'She knows,' Rita whispered. 'She's sent you this day ... '

Now the street had turned to reddish dust. Here factories rose, eyeless and higher than the trees ...

Rita said, 'I'm reading *die Bruder Grimm*. Everyone is. I'm the Goose Girl. I am a king's daughter.'

'I know it. Papa was given the book.'

'Cinderella is us – you and me ... '

In silence they walked. Then the girl said, 'I was Cinderella once. I wore a dress made of silk. It had lace at the wrists and the bodice, and ribbons weaved through the lace. It was blue.'

'Is it real still?'

'Yes.'

They stood at the factory gate and stared at the cold grey building.

'You could forget how to dream,' Rita murmured.

'Not you!'

'Nor you.'

They walked in.

The girl made her way to level one. She dropped to her hands and knees and began gathering the threads that had collected underneath the looms. From time to time she'd draw her hand over her eyes, and crawl on.

At the entrance Herr Graf was beckoning. There'd been a spill of needles on level three.

On level three Liesel was picking them up. Needles of all sizes were everywhere.

Again the girl fell to her knees and began to crawl beneath the work benches where most of the needles had fallen. For a moment she paused, heard the sound of embroiderers at work. A silence broken only by coughing or the moving of feet.

She edged her way forward and as she did a woman whose bench stood by the window called out, 'Look!'

A coach had drawn up outside the gate, and two men with leather ribbons in their hats were walking across the yard. They disappeared into the building.

On level one Herr Giersch was hurrying to meet them. The men removed their headwear and after much talking and nodding followed Herr Giersch past the weavers and across the floor to Herr Graf, who also pointed and nodded, and led the way through level two.

On level three they paused.

Heads turned as Herr Graf hurried to where the girl, on her hands and knees, was sifting through scraps. He motioned to her to follow him. She went with acceptance as she always had, not knowing what wrong it was that she might have done out of ignorance, or thoughtlessness. Or fear...

At the entrance to level three Herr Graf stopped. 'This is the one,' he said.

The girl raised her head, she stared into gold buckles, gold braid, the colour crimson. At two men ...

'She has the hair,' remarked the first. 'And the eyes are blue...'

The second carried a scroll tied with a ribbon. He held it out. 'Come here,' he said.

The girl stepped closer.

'Is that your name?'

'Yes.'

'This is for you.'

Both men bowed briefly to the girl, to Herr Giersch and Herr Graf, and walked away.

The girl clutched the thing in her hand. She looked for Rita.

Workers gathered.

'Open it,' came a voice, that of Herr Graf.

Her hands were cold, her fingers stiff. She tugged at the bow. It fell loose and unwound the ribbon. The ribbon was blue. She gazed at the twisted thread...

'Go on.'

She rolled out the scroll. On it were notes of music...
At the top were the words *Für Elise.*
It was signed Ludwig van Beethoven.